" We were both near breaking down."

See page 338.

D'RI AND I

A TALE of DARING DEEDS *in the* SECOND WAR *with the* BRITISH. Being the Memoirs of Colonel Ramon Bell, U.S.A.

By IRVING BACHELLER, author of "Eben Holden."
Illustrated by F. C. YOHN

LOTHROP PUBLISHING COMPANY
BOSTON

TO MY WIFE

PREFACE

*T*HIS is a tale of the adventurous and rugged pioneers, who, unconquered by other foes, were ever at war with the ancient wilderness, pushing the northern frontier of the white man farther and farther to the west. Early in the last century they had striped the wild waste of timber with roadways from Lake Champlain to Lake Ontario, and spotted it with sown acres wide and fair; and still, as they swung their axes with the mighty vigor of great arms, the forest fell before them.

In a long valley south of the St. Lawrence, sequestered by river, lake, and wilderness, they were slow to lose the simplicity, the dialect, and the poverty of their fathers.

Some Frenchmen of wealth and title, having fled the Reign of Terror, bought a tract of wild country there (six hundred and thirty thousand acres) and began to fill it with fine homes. It was said the great Napoleon himself would some day build a château among them. A few men of leisure built manor-houses on the river front, and so the Northern Yankee came to see something of the splendor of the far world, with contempt, as we may well imagine, for its waste of time and money.

Those days the North country was a theatre of interest and renown. Its play was a tragedy; its setting the ancient wilderness; its people of all conditions from king to farm hand. Château and cabin, trail and forest road, soldier and civilian, lake and river, now moonlit, now sunlit, now under ice and white with snow, were of the shifting scenes in that play. Sometimes the stage was overrun with cavalry and noisy with the clang of steel and the roar of the carronade.

The most important episodes herein are of history, — so romantic was the life of that time and region. The marriage is almost literally a matter of record.

A good part of the author's life has been

spent among the children of those old raiders — Yankee and Canadian — of the north and south shores of the big river. Many a tale of the camp and the night ride he has heard in the firelight of a winter's evening; long familiar to him are the ruins of a rustic life more splendid in its day than any north of Virginia. So his color is not all of books, but of inheritance and of memory as well.

The purpose of this tale is to extend acquaintance with the plain people who sweat and bled and limped and died for this Republic of ours. Darius, or "D'ri" as the woods folk called him, was a pure-bred Yankee, quaint, rugged, wise, truthful; Ramon had the hardy traits of a Puritan father, softened by the more romantic temperament of a French mother. They had no more love of fighting than they had need of it.

INTRODUCTION

FROM a letter of Captain Darius Hawkins, U. S. A., introducing Ramon Bell to the Comte de Chaumont:—

"MY DEAR COUNT: I commend to your kind offices my young friend Ramon Bell, the son of Captain Bell, a cavalry officer who long ago warmed his sword in the blood of the British on many a battle-field. The young man is himself a born soldier, as brave as he is tall and handsome. He has been but a month in the army, yet I have not before seen a man who could handle horse and sword as if they were part of him. He is a gentleman, also, and one after your own heart. I know, my dear count, you will do everything you can to further the work intrusted to him.

"Your obedient servant,
"DARIUS HAWKINS."

From a letter of Joseph Bonaparte, Comte de Survilliers, introducing his friend Colonel Ramon Bell to Napoleon III of France:—

"He has had a career romantic and interesting beyond that of any man I have met in

INTRODUCTION

America. In the late war with England he was the master of many situations most perilous and difficult. The scars of ten bullets and four sabre-thrusts are on his body. It gives me great pleasure, my dear Louis, to make you to know one of the most gallant and chivalrous of men. He has other claims upon your interest and hospitality, with which he will acquaint you in his own delightful way."

ILLUSTRATIONS

" We were both near breaking down"

Frontispiece

D'ri and I . . . . . . Page 17

" I could not for the life of me tell which of the
two charming girls I loved the better " . .

Page 110

Louise . . . . . . Page 122

" He would have fought to the death then and
there if I had but given him the word"

Page 167

" Come, now, my pretty prisoner ; it is disagreeable, but you must forgive me " . Page 183

" D'ri, shaking a bloody, tattered flag, shouted :
' We'll tek care o' the ol' brig !' " . Page 243

" Then I leave all for you " . . Page 355

D'RI AND I

 POET may be a good companion, but, so far as I know, he is ever the worst of fathers. Even as grandfather he is too near, for one poet can lay a streak of poverty over three generations. Doubt not I know whereof I speak, dear reader, for my mother's father was a poet — a French poet, too, whose lines had crossed the Atlantic long before that summer of 1770 when he came to Montreal. He died there, leaving only debts and those who had great need of a better legacy — my mother and grandmother.

As to my father, he had none of that fatal folly in him. He was a mountaineer of Vermont — a man of steely sinews that took well to the grip of a sword. He cut his way to fame in

the Northern army when the British came first
to give us battle, and a bloody way it was. I
have now a faded letter from Ethan Allen, grim
old warrior, in which he calls my father "the
best swordsman that ever straddled a horse."
He was a "gallous chap" in his youth, so said
my grandmother, with a great love of good
clothes and gunpowder. He went to Montreal,
as a boy, to be educated; took lessons in fencing, fought a duel, ran away from school, and
came home with little learning and a wife.
Punished by disinheritance, he took a farm, and
left the plough to go into battle.

I wonder often that my mother could put up
with the stress and hardship of his life, for she
had had gentle breeding, of which I knew little
until I was grown to manhood, when I came to
know also what a woman will do for the love of
her heart. I remember well those tales of
knights and ladies she used to tell me as we sat
together of an evening, and also those adventures of her own knight, my good father, in the
war with the British. My love of arms and of
a just quarrel began then.

After the war came hard times. My father

D'RI and I.

had not prospered handsomely, when, near the end of the summer of 1803, he sold his farm, and we all started West, over rough trails and roadways. There were seven of us, bound for the valley of the St. Lawrence — my father and mother, my two sisters, my grandmother, D'ri, the hired man, and myself, then a sturdy boy of ten. We had an ox-team and -cart that carried our provision, the sacred feather beds of my mother, and some few other things.

We drove with us the first flock of sheep that ever went West. There were forty of them, and they filled our days with trouble. But for our faithful dog Rover, I fear we should have lost heart and left them to the wild wolves. The cart had a low cover of canvas, and my mother and grandmother sat on the feather beds, and rode with small comfort even where the roads were level. My father let me carry my little pet rooster in a basket that hung from the cart-axle when not in my keeping. The rooster had a harder time than any of us, I fancy, for the days were hot and the roads rough. He was always panting, with open mouth and thought-ful eye, when I lifted the cover. But every day he gave us an example of cheerfulness not wholly without effect. He crowed triumphantly, betimes, in the hot basket, even when he was being tumbled about on the swamp ways. Nights I always found a perch for him on the limb of a near tree, above the reach of predatory creatures. Every morning, as the dawn showed faintly in the tree-tops, he gave it a lusty cheer, flapping his wings with all the seeming of delight. Then, often, while the echo rang, I would open my eyes and watch the light grow in the dusky cavern of the woods. He would sit dozing awhile after the first outbreak, and presently as the flood of light grew clearer, lift himself a little, take another peep at the sky, and crow again, turning his head to hear those weird, mocking roosters of the timber-land. Then, shortly, I would hear my father poking the fire or saying, as he patted the rooster: "Sass 'em back, ye noisy little brat! Thet 's right: holler. Tell D'ri it 's time t' bring some wood fer the fire."

In a few minutes the pot and kettle would be boiling and the camp all astir. We had trout and partridge and venison a-plenty for our meals, that were served in dishes of tin. Breakfast over, we packed our things. The cart went on ahead, my father bringing the oxen, while I started the sheep with D'ri.

Those sheep were as many thorns in our flesh that day we made off in the deep woods from Lake Champlain. Travel was new to them, and what with tearing through thickets and running wild in every slash, they kept us jumping. When they were leg-weary and used to travel, they began to go quietly. But slow work it was at best, ten or twelve miles a day being all we could do, for the weather was hot and our road like the way of the transgressor. Our second night in the woods we could hear the wolves howling as we camped at dusk. We built our fire near the shore of a big pond, its still water framed in the vivid green of young tamaracks. A great hill rose on the farther side of it, with galleries of timber sloping to the summit, and peopled with many birds. We huddled the sheep together in a place where the trees were thick, while father brought from the cart a coil of small rope. We wound it about the trees, so the sheep were shut in a little yard.

After supper we all sat by the fire, while D'ri told how he had been chased by wolves in the beaver country north of us.

D'ri was an odd character. He had his own way of expressing the three degrees of wonder, admiration, and surprise. "Jerushy!" — accented on the second syllable — was the positive, "Jerushy Jane!" the comparative, and "Jerushy Jane Pepper!" the superlative. Who that poor lady might be I often wondered, but never ventured to inquire. In times of stress I have heard him swear by "Judas Priest," but never more profanely. In his youth he had been a sailor on the lake, when some artist of the needle had tattooed a British jack on the back of his left hand — a thing he covered, of shame now, when he thought of it. His right hand had lost its forefinger in a sawmill. His rifle was distinguished by the name of Beeswax, — "Ol' Beeswax" he called it sometimes, — for no better reason than that it was "easy spoke an' hed a kind uv a powerful soun' tew it." He had a nose like a shoemaker's thumb : there was a deep incurve from its wide tip to his forehead. He had a large, gray, inquiring eye and

the watchful habit of the woodsman. Somewhere in the midst of a story he would pause
and peer thoughtfully into the distance, meanwhile feeling the pipe-stem with his lips, and
then resume the narrative as suddenly as he
had stopped. He was a lank and powerful
man, six feet tall in his stockings. He wore a
thin beard that had the appearance of parched
grass on his ruddy countenance. In the matter
of hair, nature had treated him with a generos-
ity most unusual. His heavy shock was
sheared off square above his neck.

That evening, as he lay on his elbow in the
firelight, D'ri had just entered the eventful field
of reminiscence. The women were washing
the dishes; my father had gone to the spring
for water. D'ri pulled up suddenly, lifted his
hat of faded felt, and listened, peering into the
dusk.

"Seems t' me them wolves is comin' nearer,"
he said thoughtfully.

Their cries were echoing in the far timber.
We all rose and listened. In a moment my
father came hurrying back with his pail of
water.

"D'ri," said he, quietly, as he threw some wood on the fire, "they smell mutton. Mek the guns ready. We may git a few pelts. There's a big bounty on 'em here 'n York State."

We all stood about the fire listening as the wolves came nearer.

"It's the sheep thet brings 'em," said my father.

"Quite a consid'able number on 'em, tew," said D'ri, as he stood cleaning the bore of his rifle.

My young sisters began to cry.

"Need n't be scairt," said father. "They won't come very near. 'Fraider of us 'n we are o' 'em, a good deal."

"Tow-w-w!" said D'ri, with a laugh. "They'll be apt t' stub ther toes 'fore they git very nigh us."

This did not quite agree with the tales he had previously been telling. I went for my sword, and buckled its belt about me, the scabbard hanging to my heels. Presently some creature came bounding over the brush. I saw him break through the wall of darkness and stop quickly in the firelight. Then D'ri brought him down with his rifle.

"Started him up back there 'n the woods a few mild," said D'ri. "He was mekin' fer this 'ere pond — thet 's what he was dewin'."

"What for?" I inquired.

"'Cause fer the reason why he knowed he would n't mek no tracks 'n the water, ner no scent," said D'ri, with some show of contempt for my ignorance.

The deer lay floundering in the briers some fifty feet away. My father ran with his knife and put him quickly out of misery. Then we hauled the carcass to clear ground.

"Let it lie where 't is fer now," said he, as we came back to the fire. Then he got our two big traps out of the cart and set them beside the carcass and covered them with leaves. The howling of the wolves had ceased. I could hear only the creaking of a dead limb high above us, and the bellow of frogs in the near pond. We had fastened the trap chains and were coming back to the fire, when the dog rose, barking fiercely; then we heard the crack of D'ri's rifle.

"More 'n fifty wolves eroun' here," he whispered as we ran up to him. "Never see sech a snag on 'em."

The sheep were stirring nervously. Near the pen a wolf lay kicking where D'ri had dropped him.

"Rest on 'em snooked off when the gun hollered," he went on, whispering as before.

My mother and grandmother sat with my sisters in the cart, hushing their murmurs of fear. Early in the evening I had tied Rover to the cart-wheel, where he was growling hotly, impatient of the leash.

"See?" said D'ri, pointing with his finger. "See 'em?— there 'n the dark by thet air big hemlock."

We could make out a dim stir in the shadows where he pointed. Presently we heard the spring and rattle of a trap. As we turned that way, the other trap took hold hard; as it sprang, we could hear a wolf yelp.

"Meks 'em holler," said D'ri, "thet ol' he-trap does, when it teks holt. Stay here by the sheep, 'n' I 'll go over 'n' give 'em somethin' fer spraint ankles."

Other wolves were swarming over the
dead deer, and the two in the traps were
snarling and snapping at them. My father
and D'ri fired at the bunch, killing one of
the captives and another — the largest wolf I
ever saw. The pack had slunk away as they
heard the rifles. Our remaining captive strug-
gled to get free, but in a moment D'ri had
brained him with an axe. He and my father
reset our traps and hauled the dead wolves
into the firelight. There they began to skin
them, for the bounty was ten dollars for each
in the new towns — a sum that made our adventure profitable. I built fires on the farther
side of the sheep, and, as they brightened, I
could see, here and there, the gleaming eyes
of a wolf in the darkness. I was up all night
heaping wood upon the fires, while D'ri and
my father skinned the wolves and dressed the
deer. I remember, as they worked, D'ri
calmed himself with the low-sung, familiar
music of : —

Li too rul I oorul I oorul I ay.

They had just finished when the cock crew.

"Holler, ye gol-dum little cuss!" D'ri

shouted as he went over to him. "Can't no snookin' wolf crack our bones fer *us*. Peeled 'em — thet 's what we done tew 'em! Tuk 'n' knocked 'em head over heels. Judas Priest! He can peck a man's finger some, can't he ?"

The light was coming, and he went off to the spring for water, while I brought the spider and pots. The great, green-roofed temple of the woods, that had so lately rung with the howl of wolves, began to fill with far wandering echoes of sweet song.

"They was a big cat over there by the spring las' night," said D'ri, as we all sat down to breakfast. "Tracks bigger 'n a griddle! Smelt the mutton, mos' likely."

"Like mutton ?" I inquired.

"Yis-sir-ee, they dew," said he. "Kind o' mince-pie fer 'em. Like deer-meat, tew. Snook eroun' the ponds efter dark. Ef they see a deer 'n the water they wallop 'im quicker 'n lightnin'; jump right in k'slap 'n' tek 'im."

We were off at sunrise, on a road that grew rougher every mile. At noon we came

to a river so swollen as to make a dangerous
ford.   After dinner my father waded in,
going hips under where the water was deep
and swift.   Then he cut a long pole and took
my mother on his shoulders and entered the
broad stream, steadying himself with the pole.
When she had got down safe on the other side,
he came back for grandmother and my sisters, and took them over in the same way.
D'ri, meanwhile, bound up the feather beds
and carried them on his head, leaving the dog
and me to tend the sheep.   All our blankets
and clothing were carried across in the same
manner.   Then I mounted the cart, with my
rooster, lashing the oxen till they took to the
stream.   They had tied the bell-wether to the
axle, and, as I started, men and dog drove
the sheep after me.   The oxen wallowed in
the deep water, and our sheep, after some hesi-
tation, began to swim.   The big cart floated
like a raft part of the way, and we landed
with no great difficulty.   Farther on, the road
became nothing better than a rude trail,
where, frequently, we had to stop and chop
through heavy logs and roll them away.   On

a steep hillside the oxen fell, breaking the tongue, and the cart tipped sidewise and rolled bottom up. My rooster was badly flung about, and began crowing and flapping as the basket settled. When I opened it, he flew out, running for his life, as if finally resolved to quit us. Fortunately, we were all walking, and nobody was hurt. My father and D'ri were busy half a day "righting up," as they called it, mending the tongue and cover, and getting the cart on its wheels and down the steep pitch.

After two days of trail travel we came out on the Chateaugay road, stopping awhile to bait our sheep and cattle on the tame grass and tender briers. It was a great joy to see the clear road, with here and there a settler's cabin, its yard aglow with the marigold, the hollyhock, and the fragrant honeysuckle. We got to the tavern at Chateaugay about dusk, and put up for the night, as becomes a Christian.

Next afternoon we came to rough roads again, camping at sundown along the shore of a noisy brook. The dog began to bark fiercely while supper was making, and scurried off into a thicket.

D'ri was stooping over, cooking the meat. He rose and listened.

"Thet air dog's a leetle scairt," said he. "Guess we better go 'n' see whut's the matter."

He took his rifle and I my sword, — I never thought of another weapon, — making off through the brush. The dog came whining to D'ri and rushing on, eager for us to follow. We hurried after him, and in a moment D'ri and the dog, who were ahead of me, halted suddenly.

"It's a painter," said D'ri, as I came up. "See 'im in thet air tree-top. I'll larrup 'im with Ol' Beeswax, then jes' like es not he'll mek some music. Better grab holt o' the dog. 'T won't dew fer 'im to git tew rambunctious, er the fust thing he knows he won't hev no insides in 'im."

I could see the big cat clinging high in the top boughs of a birch and looking calmly down at us. The tree-top swayed, quivering, as it held the great dun beast. My heart was like to smother me when D'ri raised his rifle and took aim. The dog broke away at the crack of it. The painter reeled and spat; then he came crashing through the branches, striking right and left with his fore paws to save himself. He hit the ground heavily, and the dog was on him. The painter lay as if dead. Before I could get near, Rover began shaking him by the neck. He came to suddenly, and struck the dog with a front claw, dragging him down. A loud yelp followed the blow. Quick as a flash D'ri had caught the painter by the tail and one hind leg. With a quick surge of his great, slouching shoulders, he flung him at arm's-length. The lithe body doubled on a tree trunk, quivered, and sank down, as the dog came free. In a jiffy I had run my sword through the cat's belly and made an end of him.

"Knew 'f he got them hind hooks on thet air dog he 'd rake his ribs right off," said D'ri, as he lifted his hat to scratch his head. " Would n't 'a' left nothin' but the backbone, — nut a thing, — an' thet would n't 'a' been a real fust-class one, nuther."

When D'ri was very positive, his words were well braced with negatives.

We took the painter by the hind legs and dragged him through the bushes to our camp.

The dog had a great rip across his shoulder, where the claws had struck and made furrows; but he felt a mighty pride in our capture, and never had a better appetite for a meal.

There were six more days of travel in that journey — travel so fraught with hardships, I wonder that some days we had the heart to press on. More than all, I wonder that the frail body of my mother was equal to it. But I am writing no vain record of endurance. I have written enough to suggest what moving meant in the wilderness. There is but one more color in the scenes of that journey. The fourth day after we left Chateaugay my grandmother fell ill and died suddenly there in the deep woods. We were far from any village, and sorrow slowed our steps. We pushed on, coming soon to a sawmill and a small settlement. They told us there was neither minister nor undertaker within forty miles. My father and D'ri made the coffin of planed lumber, and lined it with deerskin, and dug the grave on top of a high hill. When all was ready, my father, who had always been much given to profanity, albeit I know he was a kindly and honest man with no irreverence in his heart, called D'ri aside.

"D'ri," said he, "ye 've alwus been more proper-spoken than I hev. Say a word o' prayer?"

"Don't much b'lieve I could," said he, thoughtfully. "I hev been t' meetin', but I hain't never been no great hand fer prayin'."

"'T would n't sound right nohow fer me t' pray," said my father, "I got s' kind o' rough when I was in the army."

"'Fraid it 'll come a leetle unhandy fer me," said D'ri, with a look of embarrassment, "but I don't never shirk a tough job ef it hes t' be done."

Then he stepped forward, took off his faded hat, his brow wrinkling deep, and said, in a drawling preacher tone that had no sound of D'ri in it: "O God, tek care o' gran'ma. Help us t' go on careful, an' when we 're riled, help us t' keep er mouths shet. O God, help the ol' cart, an' the ex in pertic'lar. An' don't be no-way hard on us. Amen."

UNE was half over when we
came to our new home in the
town of Madrid — then a home
only for the foxes and the fowls
of the air and their wild kin
of the forest. The road ran through a little
valley thick with timber and rock-bound on
the north. There were four families within
a mile of us, all comfortably settled in small
log houses. For temporary use we built a
rude bark shanty that had a partition of
blankets, living in this primitive manner until my father and D'ri had felled the timber
and built a log house. We brought flour from
Malone, — a dozen sacks or more, — and while
they were building, I had to supply my mother
with fish and game and berries for the table —
a thing easy enough to do in that land of plenty.
When the logs were cut and hewn I went away,

horseback, to Canton for a jug of rum. I was all day and half the night going and coming, and fording the Grasse took me stirrups under.

Then the neighbors came to the raising — a jolly company that shouted "Hee, oh, hee!" as they lifted each heavy log to its place, and grew noisier quaffing the odorous red rum, that had a mighty good look to me, although my father would not hear of my tasting it. When it was all over, there was nothing to pay but our gratitude.

While they were building bunks, I went off to sawmill with the oxen for boards and shingles. Then, shortly, we had a roof over us and floors to walk on, and that luxury D'ri called a "pyaz," although it was not more than a mere shelf with a roof over it. We chinked the logs with moss and clay at first, putting up greased paper in the window spaces. For months we knew not the luxury of the glass pane.

That summer we "changed work" with the neighbors, and after we had helped them awhile they turned to in the clearing of our farm. We felled the trees in long, bushy windrows, heaping them up with brush and small wood when

the chopping was over. That done, we fired
the rows, filling the deep of heaven with smoke,
as it seemed to me, and lighting the night with
great billows of flame.

By mid-autumn we had cleared to the stumps
a strip half down the valley from our door.
Then we turned to on the land of our neighbors,
my time counting half, for I was sturdy and
could swing the axe to a line, and felt a joy in
seeing the chips fly. But my father kept an
eye on me, and held me back as with a leash.

My mother was often sorely tried for the
lack of things common as dirt these better days.
Frequently our only baking-powder was white
lye, made by dropping ash-cinders into water.
Our cinders were made by letting the sap of
green timber drip into hot ashes. Often deer's
tallow, bear's grease, or raccoon's oil served for
shortening, and the leaves of the wild raspberry
for tea. Our neighbors went to mill at Canton
—a journey of five days, going and coming,
with an ox-team, and beset with many difficulties. Then one of them hollowed the top of a
stump for his mortar and tied his pestle to the
bough of a tree. With a rope he drew the

bough down, which, as it sprang back, lifted the pestle that ground his grain.

But money was the rarest of all things in our neighborhood those days. Pearlash, black-salts, West India pipe-staves, and rafts of timber brought cash, but no other products of the early settler. Late that fall my mother gave a dance, a rude but hearty pleasuring that followed a long conference in which my father had a part. They all agreed to turn to, after snowfall, on the river-land, cut a raft of timber, and send it to Montreal in the spring. Our things had come, including D'ri's fiddle, so that we had chairs and bedsteads and other accessories of life not common among our neighbors. My mother had a few jewels and some fine old furniture that her father had given her, — really beautiful things, I have since come to know, — and she showed them to those simple folk with a mighty pride in her eyes.

Business over, D'ri took down his fiddle, that hung on the wall, and made the strings roar as he tuned them. Then he threw his long right leg over the other, and, as he drew the bow, his big foot began to pat the floor a good pace away. His chin lifted, his fingers flew, his bow quickened, the notes seemed to whirl and scurry, light-footed as a rout of fairies. Meanwhile the toe of his right boot counted the increasing tempo until it came up and down like a ratchet.

Darius Olin was mostly of a slow and sober manner. To cross his legs and feel a fiddle seemed to throw his heart open and put him in full gear. Then his thoughts were quick, his eyes merry, his heart was a fountain of joy. He would lean forward, swaying his head, and shouting "Yip!" as the bow hurried. D'ri was a hard-working man, but the feel of the fiddle warmed and limbered him from toe to finger. He was over-modest, making light of his skill if he ever spoke of it, and had no ear for a compliment. While our elders were dancing, I and others of my age were playing games in the kitchen — kissing-games with a rush and tumble in them, puss-in-the-corner, hunt-the-squirrel, and the like. Even then I thought I was in love with pretty Rose Merriman. She would never let me kiss her, even though I had caught her and had the right. This roundelay, sung while one was in the centre of a circling group, ready to grab at the last word, brings back to me the sweet faces, the bright eyes, the merry laughter of that night and others like it:

Oh, hap-py is th' mil-ler who lives by him-self! As th' wheel goes round, he gath-ers in 'is wealth, One hand on the hop-per and the oth-er on the bag; As the wheel goes round, he cries out, "Grab!" Oh, ain't you a lit-tle bit a-shamed o' this, Oh,

ain't you a lit-tle bit a-sham'd o' this, Oh,

ain't you a lit-tle bit a-sham'd o' this — To

ritard. D.S.:§:

stay all night for one sweet kiss? Oh, etc.

My mother gave me all the schooling I had that winter. A year later they built a school-house, not quite a mile away, where I found more fun than learning. After two years I shouldered my axe and went to the river-land with the choppers every winter morning.

My father was stronger than any of them except D'ri, who could drive his axe to the bit every blow, day after day. He had the strength of a giant, and no man I knew tried ever to cope with him. By the middle of May we began roll-ing in for the raft. As soon as they were float-ing, the logs were withed together and moored in sections. The bay became presently a quak-ing, redolent plain of timber.

When we started the raft, early in June, that summer of 1810, and worked it into the broad river with sweeps and poles, I was aboard with D'ri and six other men, bound for the big city of which I had heard so much. I was to visit the relatives of my mother and spend a year in the Collège de St. Pierre. We had a little frame house on a big platform, back of the middle section of the raft, with bunks in it, where we ate and slept and told stories. Lying on the platform, there was a large flat stone that held our fires for both cooking and comfort. D'ri called me in the dusk of the early morning, the first night out, and said we were near the Sault. I got up, rubbed my eyes, and felt a mighty thrill as I heard the roar of the great rapids and the creaking withes, and felt the lift of the speeding water. D'ri said they had broken the raft into three parts, ours being hindmost. The roaring grew louder, until my shout was as a whisper in a hurricane. The logs began to heave and fall, and waves came rushing through them. Sheets of spray shot skyward, coming down like a shower. We were shaken as by an earthquake in the rough water. Then the roar fell back of us, and the raft grew steady.

"Gin us a tough twist," said D'ri, shouting down at me — "kind uv a twist o' the bit 'n' a kick 'n the side."

It was coming daylight as we sailed into still water, and then D'ri put his hands to his mouth and hailed loudly, getting an answer out of the gloom ahead.

"Gol-dum ef it hain't the power uv a thousan' painters!" D'ri continued, laughing as he spoke. "Never see nothin' jump 'n' kick 'n' spit like thet air, 'less it hed fur on — never 'n all my born days."

D'ri's sober face showed dimly now in the dawn. His hands were on his hips; his faded felt hat was tipped sideways. His boots and trousers were quarrelling over that disputed territory between his knees and ankles. His boots had checked the invasion.

"Smooth water now," said he, thoughtfully. "Seems terrible still. Hain't a breath uv air stirrin'. Jerushy Jane Pepper! Wha' does thet mean?"

He stepped aside quickly as some bits of

bark and a small bough of hemlock fell at our feet. Then a shower of pine needles came slowly down, scattering over us and hitting the timber with a faint hiss. Before we could look up, a dry stick as long as a log fell rattling on the platform.

"Never see no sech doin's afore," said D'ri, looking upward. "Things don't seem t' me t' be actin' eggzac'ly nat'ral — nut jest es I 'd like t' see 'em."

As the light came clearer, we saw clouds heaped black and blue over the tree-tops in the southwest. We stood a moment looking. The clouds were heaping higher, pulsing with light, roaring with thunder. What seemed to be a flock of pigeons rose suddenly above the far forest, and then fell as if they had all been shot. A gust of wind coasted down the still ether, fluttering like a rag and shaking out a few drops of rain.

"Look there!" I shouted, pointing aloft.

"Hark!" said D'ri, sharply, raising his hand of three fingers.

We could hear a far sound like that of a great wagon rumbling on a stony road.

"The Almighty's whippin' his hosses," said D'ri. "Looks es ef he wus plungin' 'em through the woods 'way yender. Look a' thet air sky."

The cloud-masses were looming rapidly. They had a glow like that of copper.

"Tryin' t' put a ruf on the world," my companion shouted. "Swingin' ther hammers hard on the rivets."

A little peak of green vapor showed above the sky-line. It loomed high as we looked. It grew into a lofty column, reeling far above the forest. Below it we could see a mighty heaving in the tree-tops. Something like an immense bird was hurtling and pirouetting in the air above them. The tower of green looked now like a great flaring bucket hooped with fire and overflowing with darkness. Our ears were full of a mighty voice out of the heavens. A wind came roaring down some tideway of the air like water in a flume. It seemed to tap the sky. Before I could gather my thoughts we were in a torrent of rushing air, and the raft had begun to heave and toss. I felt D'ri take my hand in his. I could just see his face, for the morning had turned dark suddenly. His lips were moving, but I could hear nothing he said. Then he lay flat, pulling me down. Above and around were all the noises that ever came to the ear of man — the beating of drums, the bellowing of cattle, the crash of falling trees, the shriek of women, the rattle of machinery, the roar of waters, the crack of rifles, the blowing of trumpets, the braying of asses, and sounds the like of which I have never heard and pray God I may not hear again, one and then another dominating the mighty chorus. Behind us, in the gloom, I could see, or thought I could see, the reeling mass of green ploughing the water, like a ship with chains of gold flashing over bulwarks of fire. In a moment something happened of which I have never had any definite notion. I felt the strong arm of D'ri clasping me tightly. I heard the thump and roll and rattle of the logs heaping above us; I felt the water washing over me; but I could see nothing. I knew the raft had doubled; it would fall and grind our bones: but I made no effort to save myself. And thinking how helpless I felt is the last I remember of the great windfall of June 3, 1810, the path of which may be seen now, fifty years after that memorable day, and I suppose it will be visible long after my bones have crumbled. I thought I had been sleeping when I came to; at least, I had dreamed. I was in some place where it was dark and still. I could hear nothing but the drip of water; I could feel the arm of D'ri about me, and I called to him, and then I felt him stir.

"Thet you, Ray?" said he, lifting his head.

"Yes," I answered. "Where are we?"

"Judas Priest! I ain' no idee. Jes' woke up. Been a-layin' here tryin' t' think. Ye hurt?"

"Guess not," said I.

"Ain't ye got no pains or aches nowhere 'n yer body?"

"Head aches a little," said I.

He rose to his elbow, and made a light with his flint and tinder, and looked at me.

"Got a goose-egg on yer for'ard," said he, and then I saw there was blood on his face.

"Ef it hed n't been fer the withes they 'd 'a' ground us t' powder."

We were lying alongside the little house, and the logs were leaning to it above us.

"Jerushy Jane Pepper!" D'ri exclaimed, rising to his knees. "'S whut I call a twister."

He began to whittle a piece of the splintered platform. Then he lit a shaving.

"They's ground here," said he, as he began to kindle a fire, "ground a-plenty right under us."

The firelight gave us a good look at our cave under the logs. It was about ten feet long and probably half as high. The logs had crashed through the side of the house in one or two places, and its roof was a wreck.

"Hungry?" said D'ri, as he broke a piece of board on his knee.

"Yes," I answered.

"So 'm I," said he, "hungrier 'n a she-wolf. They's some bread 'n' ven'son there 'n the house; we better try t' git 'em."

An opening under the logs let me around the house corner to its door. I was able to work my way through the latter, although it was choked with heavy timbers. Inside I could hear the wash of the river, and through its shattered window on the farther wall I could see between the heaped logs a glow of sunlit water. I handed our axe through a break in the wall, and then D'ri cut away some of the baseboards and joined me. We had our meal cooking in a few minutes — our dinner, really, for D'ri said it was near noon. Having eaten, we crawled out of the window, and then D'ri began to pry the logs apart.

"Ain't much 'fraid o' their tumblin' on us," said he. "They 're withed so they 'll stick together."

We got to another cave under the logs, at the water's edge, after an hour of crawling and prying. A side of the raft was in the water.

"Got t' dive," said D'ri, "an' swim fer daylight."

A long swim it was, but we came up in clear water, badly out of breath. We swam around the timber, scrambling over a dead cow, and up-shore. The ruined raft was torn and tumbled into a very mountain of logs at the edge of the water. The sun was shining clear, and the air was still. Limbs of trees, bits of torn cloth, a broken hay-rake, fragments of wool, a wagon-wheel, and two dead sheep were scattered along the shore. Where we had seen the whirlwind coming, the sky was clear, and beneath it was a great gap in the woods, with ragged walls of evergreen. Here and there in the gap a stub was standing, trunk and limbs naked.

"Jerushy Jane Pepper!" D'ri exclaimed, with a pause after each word. "It's cut a swath wider 'n this river. Don't b'lieve a mouse could 'a' lived where the timber 's down over there."

Our sweepers and the other sections of the raft were nowhere in sight.

E left the logs, and walked to Cornwall, and took a sloop down the river. It was an American boat, bound for Quebec with pipe-staves. It had put in at Cornwall when the storm began. The captain said that the other sections of our raft had passed safely. In the dusk of the early evening a British schooner brought us to.

"Wonder what that means?" said the skipper, straining his eyes in the dusk.

A small boat, with three officers, came alongside. They climbed aboard, one of them carrying a lantern. They were armed with swords and pistols. We sat in silence around the cockpit. They scanned each of us carefully in the light of the lantern. It struck me as odd they should look so closely at our hands.

"Wha' d' ye want?" the skipper demanded.

"This man," said one of them, pointing to D'ri. "He's a British sailor. We arrest him —"

He got no farther. D'ri's hand had gone out like the paw of a painter and sent him across the cockpit. Before I knew what was up, I saw the lank body of D'ri leaping backward into the river. I heard a splash and a stroke of his long arms, and then all was still. I knew he was swimming under water to get away. The officers made for their boat. My blood was up, and I sprang at the last of them, giving him a hard shove as he was climbing over, so that he fell on the boat, upsetting it. They had business enough then for a little, and began hailing for help. I knew I had done a foolish thing, and ran forward, climbing out upon the bowsprit, and off with my coat and vest, and dived into the dark water. I swam under as long as I could hold my breath, and then came up quietly, turning on my back in the quick current, and floating so my face only was above water. It had grown dark, and I could see nothing but the glimmer of the stars above me. My boots were heavy and dragged hard. I was going fast with the swift water, for at first I had heard a great hubbub on the schooner; but now its voices had grown faint. Other sounds were filling my ear.

After dark it is weird business to be swimming in strange water — the throne of mystery, of a thousand terrors. It is as if one's grave, full of the blackness of the undiscovered country, were pursuing him and ever yawning beneath his body. And that big river is the very tiger of waters, now stealing on pussy-footed, now rushing with cat-like swiftness, hissing and striking with currents that have in them mighty sinews. I was now companion of those cold-mouthed monsters of the river bottom, many of which I had seen. What if one should lay hold on me and drag me under? Then I thought of rapids that might smother me with their spray or dash me to hidden rocks. Often I lifted my ears, marvelling at the many voices of the river. Sometimes I thought I heard a roaring like that of the Sault, but it was only a ripple growing into fleecy waves that rocked me as in a cradle. The many sounds were above, below,

and beside me, some weird and hollow and un-
earthly. I could hear rocks rolling over in their
sleep on the bottom, and, when the water was
still, a sound like the cropping of lily-pads
away off on the river-margin. The bellowing
of a cow terrified me as it boomed over the
sounding sheet of water. The river rang like
a mighty drum when a peal of far thunder
beat upon it. I put out my hands to take a
stroke or two as I lay on my back, and felt
something floating under water. The feel of
it filled me with horror. I swam faster; it was
at my heels. I knew full well what my hand
had touched — a human head floating face
downward : I could feel the hair in my fingers.
I turned and swam hard, but still it followed me.
My knees hit upon it, and then my feet. Again
and again I could feel it as I kicked. Its hand
seemed to be clutching my trousers. I thought
I should never get clear of the ghastly thing. I
remember wondering if it were the body of poor
D'ri. I turned aside, swimming another way,
and then I felt it no more.

In the dead of the night I heard suddenly a
kind of throbbing in the breast of the river. It

grew to a noisy heart-beat as I listened. Again and again I heard it, striking, plashing, like a footfall, and coming nearer. Somehow I got the notion of a giant, like those of whom my mother had told me long ago, striding in the deep river. I could hear his boots dripping as he lifted them. I got an odd fear that he would step on me. Then I heard music and lifted my ears above water. It was a voice singing in the distance, — it must have been a mile off, — and what I had taken for a near footfall shrank away. I knew now it was the beat of oars in some far bay.

A long time after I had ceased to hear it, something touched my shoulder and put me in a panic. Turning over, I got a big mouthful of water. Then I saw it was a gang of logs passing me, and quickly caught one. Now, to me the top side of a log was as easy and familiar as a rocking-chair. In a moment I was sitting comfortably on my captive. A bit of rubbish, like that the wind had sown, trailed after the gang of logs. I felt it over, finding a straw hat and a piece of board some three feet long, with which latter I paddled vigorously.

It must have been long past midnight when I came to an island looming in the dark ahead. I sculled for it, stranding on a rocky beach, and alighted, hauling the log ashore. The moon came out as I stood wringing my trouser legs. I saw the island rose high and narrow and was thickly wooded. I remember saying something to myself, when I heard a quick stir in the bushes near me. Looking up, I saw a tall figure. Then came a familiar voice : —

"Thet you, Ray? Judas Priest!"

I was filled with joy at the sight of D'ri, and put my arms about him and lifted him off his feet, and, faith! I know my eyes were wet as my trousers. Then, as we sat down, I told him how I had taken to the river.

"Lucky ye done it!" said he. "Jerushy Jane! It is terrible lucky! They'd 'a' tuk ye sartin. Somebody see thet jack on the back o' my hand, there 'n Cornwall, 'n' put 'em efter me. But I was bound 'n' determined they'd never tek me alive, never! Ef I ever dew any fightin', 't ain't a-goin' t' be fer England, nut by a side o' sole-leather. I med up my mind I 'd begin the war right then an' there."

my father and I and the children. He pulled up a moment, his horse lathered to the ears.

"Injuns!" he shouted. "Git out o' here quick 'n' mek fer the Corners! Ye 'll be all massacreed ef ye don't."

Then he whacked the wet flank of his horse with a worn beech bough, and off he went.

We ran to the house in a great panic. I shall never forget the crying of the children. Indians had long been the favorite bugbear of the border country. Many a winter's evening we had sat in the firelight, fear-faced, as my father told of the slaughter in Cherry Valley; and, with the certainty of war, we all looked for the red hordes of Canada to come, in paint and feathers.

"Ray," my father called to me, as he ran, "ketch the cow quick an' bring 'er 'long."

I caught her by the horn and brought her to the door quickly. Mother was throwing some clothes into a big bundle. Father met me with a feather bed in his arms. He threw it over the back of the cow and bound it on with a bed-cord. That done, he gave me the leading-rope to tie about her horns. The hoofs of the flying horse were hardly out of hearing when we were all in the road. My mother carried the baby, and my father his sword and rifle and one of the little ones. I took the three older children and set them on the feather bed that was bound to the back of the cow. They clung to the bed-cord, their hair flying, as the old cow ran to keep up with us, for at first we were all running. In a moment we could hear the voices of people coming behind. One of the women was weeping loudly as she ran. At the first cross-road we saw Arv Law and his family coming, in as great a hurry as we. Arv had a great pike-pole in his hand. Its upper end rose twenty feet above his head.

"What ye goin' t' dew with thet?" my father asked him.

"Goin' t' run it through the fust Injun I see," said he. "I 've broke the lock o' my gun."

There was a crowd at Jerusalem Four Corners when we got there. Every moment some family was arriving in a panic — the men, like my father, with guns and babies and baskets. The women, with the young, took refuge at once in the tavern, while the men surrounded

it. Inside the line were youths, some oddly
armed with slings or clubs or cross-guns. I
had only the sword my father gave me and a
mighty longing to use it. Arv Law rested an
end of his pike-pole and stood looking anxiously
for "red devils" among the stumps of the farther clearing. An old flint-lock, on the shoulder
of a man beside him, had a barrel half as long
as the pole. David Church was equipped with
axe and gun, that stood at rest on either side of
him.

Evening came, and no sign of Indians.
While it was growing dusk I borrowed a pail
of the innkeeper and milked the cow, and
brought the pail, heaped with froth, to my
mother, who passed brimming cups of milk
among the children. As night fell, we boys,
more daring than our fathers, crept to the edge
of the timber and set the big brush-heaps afire,
and scurried back with the fear of redmen at
our heels. The men were now sitting in easy
attitudes and had begun to talk.

"Don't b'lieve there's no Injuns comin',"
said Bill Foster. "Ef they wus they'd come."

"'Cordin' t' my observation," said Arv Law,

looking up at the sky, "Injuns mos' gen'ally comes when they git ready."

"An' 't ain't when yer ready t' hev 'em, nuther," said Lon Butterfield.

"B'lieve they come up 'n' peeked out o' the bushes 'n' see Arv with thet air pike-pole, 'n' med up their minds they hed n't better run up ag'in' it," said Bill Foster. "Scairt 'em — thet 's whut 's th' matter."

"Man 'et meks light o' this pole oughter hev t' carry it," said Arv, as he sat impassively resting it upon his knee.

"One thin' 's sure," said Foster; "ef Arv sh'u'd cuff an Injun with thet air he 'll squ'sh 'im."

"Squ'sh 'im!" said Arv, with a look of disgust. "'T ain't med t' squ'sh with. I cal'late t' p'int it at 'em 'n' jab."

And so, as the evening wore away and sleep hushed the timid, a better feeling came over us. I sat by Rose Merriman on the steps, and we had no thought of Indians. I was looking into her big hazel eyes, shining in the firelight, and thinking how beautiful she was. And she, too, was looking into my eyes, while we whispered

together, and the sly minx read my thoughts, I
know, by the look of her.

Great flames were now leaping high as the
timber-tops at the edge of the clearing. A dead
spruce caught fire as we were looking. The
flames threw over it a lacy, shimmering, crac-
kling net of gold. Then suddenly it burst into a
red, leaping tower. A few moments, and the
cavern of the woods, along the timber side, was
choked with fire. The little hamlet had become
a spring of light in the darkness. We could see
the stumps and houses far afield, as if it had
been noonday. Suddenly we all jumped to our
feet. A wild yell came echoing through the
woods.

"There they be!" said Asher Eastman, as
he cocked his gun. "I tol' ye so."

As a matter of fact, he had told us nothing of
the kind. He was the one man who had said
nothing.

Arv Law stood erect, his pike-pole poised in
both hands, and we were all ready for action.
We could hear the rattle of many hoofs on the
road. As soon as the column showed in the
firelight, Bill Foster up with his musket and

pulled the trigger. I could hear the shot scatter on stump and stone. Every man had his gun to his eye.

"Wait till they come nearer," said Asher Eastman.

The Indians had halted. Far behind them we could hear the wild hallooing of many voices. In a moment we could see those on horseback go galloping off in the direction whence they had come. Back in the house a number of the women were praying. My mother came out, her face whiter than I had ever seen it before, and walked to my father, and kissed him without ever saying a word. Then she went back into the house.

"Scairt?" I inquired, turning to Rose, who now stood beside me.

"I should think I was," she whispered. "I'm all of a tremble."

"If anything happens, I'd like something to remember you by."

"What?" she whispered.

I looked at her beautiful red lips. She had never let me kiss them.

"A kiss, if nothing more," I answered.

She gave me a kiss then that told me something of what was in her heart, and went away into the house.

"Goin' t' surround us," said Arv Law — "thet's whut's th' matter."

"Mus' be ready t' rassle 'em any minute," said Asher Eastman, as he sidled over to a little group.

A young man came out of the house and took his place in line with a big squirt-gun and a pail of steaming-hot water.

The night wore on; our fires burned low. As the approaching day began to light the clearing, we heard a sound that brought us all to our feet. A burst of bugle notes went chasing over the timber-land to the tune of "Yankee Doodle." We looked at one another in surprise. Then there came a thunder of hoofs in the distance, the ragged outline of a troop of cavalry.

"Soldiers!" said Arv, as he raised his pike.

"The British?" somebody asked.

"Dunno," said he. "Ain' no Injuns, I don't b'lieve."

A troop of cavalry was approaching at a gallop. They pulled up a few rods away and jammed into a big crescent of rearing, trampling horses. We could see they were American soldiers. We all lowered our guns.

"Who are you?" one of them shouted.

"Citizens," my father answered.

"Why are you armed?"

"To fight Injuns."

A chorus of laughter came from the cavalry. They loosed rein, letting their horses advance.

"My dear man," said one of them, a big shako on his head, "there ain't an Indian 'tween here an' St. Regis. We thought you were British, an' it's lucky we did n't charge in the dark; we'd have cut you all to pieces before we knew who you were."

A body of infantry was marching down the pike. They were the volunteers of Captain Darius Hawkins, on their way to Ogdensburg, with an escort of cavalry from Sackett's Harbor. The scare was over. Women came out, laughing and chattering. In a few moments they were all in the road, going home — men, women, and children.

I enlisted with Captain Hawkins, and hurried to the house, and packed my things, and bade them all good-by.

FOLLOWED the camp and took my place in the ranks at Ogdensburg. We went immediately into barracks — a structure long and low and weatherstained, overlooking the St. Lawrence. There was a fine level field in front of it, and a flag waving at the top of a high staff. The men cheered lustily that afternoon as they passed it, where stood General Jacob Brown, his cocked hat in his hand — a splendid figure of a man. My delight in the life of a soldier began that hour, and has never left me.

There was a lot of horse-play that night, in which some of the green boys were roughly handled. They told me, I remember, that all new recruits had to fight a duel; but when they gave me the choice of weapons I was well content. I had the sure eye of my father, and the

with.   He kept his temper and smoked thoughtfully, and took it all in good part.   The night
after he came they put him on guard duty — a
greenhorn, with no knowledge of any orders but
gee and haw.   They told him he should allow
nobody to pass him while on duty, but omitted
to mention the countersign.   They instructed
him in the serious nature of his task, adding
that his failure to comply with orders would
incur the penalty of death.   D'ri looked very
sober as he listened.   No man ever felt a
keener sense of responsibility.   They intended,
I think, to cross the lines and take his gun
away and have fun with him, but the countersign would have interfered with their plans.

D'ri went to his post a little after sundown.
The guard was posted.   The sergeant, with his
party of six, started back to the guard-house,
but they never got there.   They went as far as
D'ri.   He stood with his gun raised.

"Come another step," said he, "an' I'll let
the moonlight through ye."

They knew he meant it, and they stood still.

"Come for'ard — one et a time," said D'ri.
"Drop yer guns 'n' set down.   Ye look tired."

They did as he commanded, for they could see he meant business, and they knew he had the right to kill.

Another man came along shortly.

"Halt! Who comes there?" D'ri demanded.

"Friend with the countersign," he replied.

"Can't fool me," said D'ri. "Come up here 'n' set down 'n' mek yerself t' hum. Drop yer gun fust. Drop it, er I 'll drop you."

He dropped his gun promptly and accepted the invitation to sit down. This last man had some arguments to offer, but D'ri stood sternly and made no reply.

At eleven o'clock Captain Hawkins sent out inquiries for the sergeant of the guard and his relief. He could find nobody who had seen them since dark. A corporal was also missing. The captain sent a man to look for them. He got as far as D'ri and sat down. They waited for him in vain. The captain stood looking into the darkness and wondering about his men. He conferred with Adjutant Church. Then he set out with two men to go the rounds. They got as far as D'ri.

"Halt! Who comes there?" he demanded.

"Grand rounds," was the answer of the captain.

"Lay down yer arms," said D'ri, "an' come up here 'n' set down."

"Haven't time," said the captain, failing at first to grasp the situation.

"You tek time, er I'll put a hole 'n yer jacket," said D'ri.

One of the privates turned quickly and ran. D'ri sent a shot after him, that only grazed a leg, and he kept on. Then D'ri gave all attention to his new prisoners. They could see no amusement in dodging bullets; they threw their arms on the side-hill and sat down with the others.

The captain swore as he submitted.

"Don't rile yerself," said D'ri; "you need rest."

"No, I don't, nuther," said the captain.

"Ye'll hev t' hev it, anyway," said D'ri.

"This beats h—!" the captain answered, with a laugh.

A feeling of alarm began to spread. The adjutant was standing in a group of men at headquarters soon after midnight. They were ears under in the mystery. The escaped soldier came running toward them out of the dark. He was breathing heavily; his leg was bleeding and sore.

"Wall, what is it?" the adjutant demanded.

"D'ri!" the man gasped, and dropped down exhausted.

"D'ri?" the officer inquired.

"D'ri!" the man repeated. "It's thet air man they call D'ri. He's roped in everybody thet come his way. They're all settin' on the hill up there beside him. Won't let a man move when he gits him."

The adjutant snickered as he spat an oath. He was made of iron, that man Church.

"Post a guard around him," said he, turning to an officer. "The dem fool'd tek the hull garrison ef we did n't. I'll go 'n' try t' pull him off his perch."

"He'll lay ye up," said the returned private, baring his bloody leg. "Eff ye try t' fool with *him* ye'll limp. See what he done t' me."

The adjutant swore again.

"Go t' the hospital," he commanded.

Then he strode away, but he did not return that night.

The moon was shining as the adjutant came in sight and hailed the group of prisoners.

"What ye settin' there fer?" he shouted.

"You'll know 'n a minute," said one of them.

"Halt! Who comes there?" D'ri demanded.

"Friend with—"

"Don't ye purten' t' be my friend," D'ri answered. "'T won't work. Come up here 'n' set down."

"Stop foolin', man," said the adjutant.

"I ain't a-foolin'."

"He ain't a-foolin'; he means business," said one of the prisoners.

"Don't ye tamper with me. I'll teach you—" the adjutant threatened.

"Ain't a-goin' t' tamper with ye a minute," said D'ri. "If ye don't set down here quick, I'll put a hole in ye."

"Lunatic! wha' d' ye mean?"

"I mean t' turn ye out t' grass a leetle while," D'ri answered soberly. "Ye look tired."

The officer made at him, but in a flash D'ri had knocked him down with his musket. The adjutant rose and, with an oath, joined the others.

"Dunno but he'll tek the hull garrison 'fore sunrise," he muttered. "Let 'em come—might es well hev comp'ny."

A little before daylight a man sick in the hospital explained the situation. He had given D'ri his orders. They brought him out on a stretcher. The orders were rescinded, the prisoners released.

Captain Hawkins, hot to his toes with anger, took D'ri to headquarters. General Brown laughed heartily when he heard the facts, and told D'ri he was made of the right stuff.

"These greenhorns are not nice to play with," he said. "They're like some guns — loaded when you don't expect it. We've had enough skylarking."

And when the sick man came out of hospital he went to the guard-house.

After we had shown our mettle the general always had a good word for D'ri and me, and he put us to the front in every difficult enterprise.

E had been four months in Ogdensburg, waiting vainly for some provocation to fight. Our own drilling was the only sign of war we could see on either side of the river. At first many moved out of the village, but the mill was kept running, and after a little they began to come back. The farms on each side of the river looked as peaceful as they had ever looked. The command had grown rapidly. Thurst Miles of my own neighborhood had come to enlist shortly after D'ri and I enlisted, and was now in my company.

In September, General Brown was ordered to the Western frontier, and Captain Forsyth came to command us. Early in the morning of October 2, a man came galloping up the shore with a warning, saying that the river

was black with boats a little way down. Some
of us climbed to the barracks roof, from which
we could see and count them. There were
forty, with two gunboats. Cannonading began
before the town was fairly awake. First a big
ball went over the house-tops, hitting a cupola
on a church roof and sending bell and timbers
with a crash into somebody's dooryard. Then
all over the village hens began to cackle and
children to wail. People came running out of
doors half dressed. A woman, gathering chips
in her dooryard, dropped them, lifted her dress
above her head, and ran for the house. Unable
to see her way, she went around in a wide circle
for a minute or two, while the soldiers were
laughing. Another ball hit a big water-tank
on top of the lead-works. It hurled broken
staves and a big slop of water upon the house-
tops, and rolled a great iron hoop over roofs
into the street below, where it rolled on, chasing
a group of men, who ran for their lives before
it. The attack was an odd sort of comedy all
through, for nobody was hurt, and all were
frightened save those of us who were amused.
Our cannon gave quick reply, and soon the

British stopped firing and drew near. We knew that they would try to force a landing, and were ready for them. We drove them back, when they put off, and that was the end of it.

Next came the fight on the ice in February — a thing not highly creditable to us, albeit we were then but a handful and they were many. But D'ri and I had no cause for shame of our part in it. We wallowed to our waists in the snow, and it was red enough in front of us. But the others gave way there on the edge of the river, and we had to follow. We knew when it was time to run; we were never in the rear rank even then. We made off with the others, although a sabre's point had raked me in the temple, and the blood had frozen on me, and I was a sight to scare a trooper. Everybody ran that day, and the British took the village, holding it only twenty-four hours. For our part in it D'ri got the rank of corporal and I was raised from lieutenant to captain. We made our way to Sackett's Harbor, where I went into hospital for a month.

Then came a galling time of idleness. In

June we went with General Brown — D'ri and I and Thurst Miles and Seth Alexander and half a dozen others — down the river to the scene of our first fighting at Ogdensburg, camping well back in the woods. It was the evening of the 27th of June that the general sent for me. He was at the mansion of Mr. Parish, where he had been dining. He was sitting in his dress-suit. His dark side-whiskers and hair were brushed carefully forward. His handsome face turned toward me with a kindly look.

"Bell," said he, "I wish to send you on very important business. You have all the qualities of a good scout. You know the woods. You have courage and skill and tact. I wish you to start immediately, go along the river to Morristown, then cut over into the Black River country and deliver this letter to the Comte de Chaumont, at the Château Le Ray, in Leraysville. If you see any signs of the enemy, send a report to me at once. I shall be here three days. Take Alexander, Olin, and Miles with you; they are all good men. When your letter is delivered, report at the Harbor as soon as possible."

I was on the road with my party in half an hour. We were all good horsemen. D'ri knew the shortest way out of the woods in any part of the north country. Thurst had travelled the forest from Albany to Sackett's Harbor, and was the best hunter that ever trod a trail in my time. The night was dark, but we rode at a gallop until we had left the town far behind us. We were at Morristown before midnight, pounding on the door of the Red Tavern. The landlord stuck his head out of an upper window, peering down at us by the light of a candle.

"Everything quiet?" I asked.

"Everything quiet," said he. "Crossed the river yesterday. Folks go back 'n' forth 'bout the same as ever. Wife's in Elizabethtown now, visiting."

We asked about the west roads and went on our way. Long before daylight we were climbing the steep road at Rossie to the inn of the Travellers' Rest — a tavern famous in its time, that stood half up the hill, with a store, a smithy, and a few houses grouped about it. We came up at a silent walk on a road cushioned with sawdust. D'ri rapped on the door until I thought he had roused the whole village. At last a man came to the upper window. He, too, inspected us with a candle. Then he opened the door and gave us a hearty welcome. We put up our horses for a bite, and came into the bar.

"Anything new?" I inquired.

"They say the British are camped this side of the river, north of us," said he, "with a big tribe of Injuns. Some of their cavalry came within three miles of us to-day. Everybody scairt t' death."

He began to set out a row of glasses.

"What 'll ye hev?" he inquired.

"Guess I 'll tip a little blue ruin int' me," said D'ri, with a shiver; "'s a col' night."

Seth and I called for the same.

"An' you?" said the landlord, turning to Thurst.

"Wal," said the latter, as he stroked his thin beard, "when I tuk the pledge I swore et I hoped t' drop dead 'fore I see myself tek another drink. I 'm jest goin' t' shet my eyes 'n' hold out my glass. I don' care what ye gi' me s' long es it 's somethin' powerful."

We ate crackers and cheese while the land-lord was telling of the west roads and the probable location of the British. He stopped suddenly, peered over my shoulder, and blew out the candle. We could hear a horse neigh-ing in the yard.

"Some one et the window," he whispered. Then he ran to the door and drew the bolt. "Ain' much idee who 't is," he added, peering out of the window. "By gosh! more 'n a dozen folks out here, soldiers tew, most uv 'em on horseback. Come quick."

We followed him upstairs, in the dark, as they began to pound the door. From the yard a light flashed up. They were evidently build-ing a fire so that they would have better shoot-ing if we came out.

"May set the house afire," said the landlord.

He quickly unwound a big hose that ran up to a tank in the peak above us.

"Plenty o' water?" D'ri whispered.

"Rivers uv it," said the landlord. "Tank 's connected with the reservoir o' the lead-works on the hill up there. Big wooden pipe comes in the gable-end."

"Turn 'er on," said D'ri, quickly, "an' let me hev thet air hose."

The landlord ran up a ladder. D'ri stuck the hose out of the window. The stream shot away with a loud hiss. I stood by and saw the jet of water leap forth as big as a pikestaff. A man went off his horse, sprawling as if he had been hit with a club. The jet leaped quickly from one to another, roaring on man and beast. There was a mighty scurry. Horses went headlong down the hill, some dragging their riders. In the silence of the night, bedlam had broken loose. The shouting men, the plunging horses, the stream of water roaring on rock and road, woke the village. Men came running from behind the house to see what had happened, then rushed after their horses. Some fell cursing as the water hit them. The landlord put his mouth to my ear.

"Mek fer yer hosses," he hissed.

We were below-stairs and out of the door in a jiffy. Two men fled before us at the stable, scrambled over the fence, and went tumbling downhill. We bridled our horses with all speed, leaped upon them, and went rushing

down the steep road, our swords in hand, like
an avalanche. They tried to stop us at the foot
of the hill, but fell away as we came near. I
could hear the snap of their triggers in passing.
Only one pistol-shot came after us, and that
went high.

"Guess their ammunition's a leetle wet," said
D'ri, with a shout that turned into laughter as
we left the British behind us.

A party of four or five mounted and gave
chase; but our powder was a bit drier than
theirs, and for a time we raked the road with
our bullets. What befell them I know not.
I only know that they held up and fell out of
hearing.

Crossing a small river at daylight, we took
the bed of it, making our way slowly for half
a mile or so into the woods. There we built
a fire, and gave the horses half the feed in our
saddle-bags, and ate our mess on a flat rock.

"Never hed no sech joemightyful time es
thet afore," said D'ri, as he sat down, laughing,
and shook his head. "Jerushy Jane! Did n't
we come down thet air hill! Luk slidin' on a
greased pole."

"Comin' so luk the devil they did n't dast git 'n er way," said Thurst.

"We wus all rippin' th' air 'ith them air joemightyful big sabres, tew," D'ri went on. "Hed a purty middlin' sharp edge on us. Stuck out luk a haystack right 'n' left."

He began bringing wood as he sang the chorus of his favorite ballad:—

Li toorul I oorul I oorul I ay, etc.

Thurst knew a trail that crossed the river near by and met the Caraway Pike a few miles beyond. Having eaten, I wrote a despatch to be taken back by Thurst as soon as we reached the pike. Past ten o'clock we turned into a rough road, where the three of us went one way and Thurst another.

I rode slowly, for the horses were nearly fagged. I gave them an hour's rest when we put up for dinner. Then we pushed on, coming in sight of the Château Le Ray at sundown. A splendid place it was, the castle of gray stone fronting a fair stretch of wooded lawn, cut by a brook that went splashing over rocks near by, and sent its velvet voice through wood and field. A road of fine gravel led through groves of beech and oak and pine to a grassy terrace under the castle walls. A servant in livery came to meet us at the door, and went to call his master. Presently a tall, handsome man, with black eyes and iron-gray hair and mustache, came down a path, clapping his hands.

"Welcome, gentlemen! It is the Captain Bell?" said he, with a marked accent, as he came to me, his hand extended. "You come from Monsieur the General Brown, do you not?"

"I do," said I, handing him my message.

He broke the seal and read it carefully.

"I am glad to see you — ver' glad to see you!" said he, laying his hands upon my shoulders and giving me a little shake.

Two servants went away with D'ri and Seth and the horses.

"Come, captain," said my host, as he led the way. "You are in good time for dinner."

We entered a great triangular hall, lighted by wide windows above the door, and candelabra of shining brass that hung from its high ceiling. There were sliding doors of polished wood on each side of it. A great stairway filled the point of the triangle. I was shown to my room, which was as big as a ball-room, it seemed to me, and grandly furnished: no castle of my dreams had been quite so fine. The valet of the count looked after me, with offers of new linen and more things than I could see use for. He could not speak English, I remember, and I addressed him in the good French my mother had taught me.

The kind of life I saw in this grand home was not wholly new to me, for both my mother and father had known good living in their youth, and I had heard much of it. I should have been glad of a new uniform; but after I had had my bath and put on the new shirt and collar the valet had brought me, I stood before the long pier-glass and saw no poor figure of a man.

The great dining-hall of the count was lighted with many candles when we came in to dinner. It had a big fireplace, where logs were blazing, for the night had turned cool, and a long table with a big epergne of wrought silver, filled with roses, in its centre. A great silken rug lay un-

der the table, on a polished floor, and the walls
were hung with tapestry. I sat beside the count,
and opposite me was the daughter of the Sieur
Louis François de Saint-Michel, king's forester
under Louis XVI. Thérèse, the handsome
daughter of the count, sat facing him at the
farther end of the table, and beside her was
the young Marquis de Gonvello. M. Pidgeon,
the celebrated French astronomer, Moss Kent,
brother of the since famous chancellor, the
Sieur Michel, and the Baroness de Ferré, with
her two wards, the Misses Louise and Louison
de Lambert, were also at dinner. These young
ladies were the most remarkable of the company; their beauty was so brilliant, so fascinating, it kindled a great fire in me the moment I
saw it. They said little, but seemed to have
much interest in all the talk of the table. I
looked at them more than was polite, I am sure,
but they looked at me quite as often. They had
big, beautiful brown eyes, and dark hair fastened high with jewelled pins, and profiles like
those of the fair ladies of Sir Peter Lely, so
finely were they cut. One had a form a bit
fuller and stronger than the other's, but they

were both as tall and trim as a young beech,
with lips cherry-red and cheeks where one
could see faintly the glow of their young blood.
Their gowns were cut low, showing the grace-
ful lines of neck and shoulder and full bosom.
I had seen pretty girls, many of them, but few
high-bred, beautiful young women. The moment I saw these two some new and mighty
force came into me. There were wine and wit
a-plenty at the count's table, and other things
that were also new to me, and for which I
retained perhaps too great a fondness.

The count asked me to tell of our journey,
and I told the story with all the spirit I could
put into my words. I am happy to say it did
seem to hit the mark, for I was no sooner done
with our adventure than the ladies began to
clap their hands, and the Misses de Lambert
had much delight in their faces when the baroness retold my story in French.

Dinner over, the count invited me to the
smoking-room, where, in a corner by ourselves,
I had some talk with him. He told me of his
father — that he had been a friend of Franklin,
that he had given a ship and a cargo of gun-

powder to our navy in '76. Like others I had met under his roof, the count had seen the coming of the Reign of Terror in France, and had fled with his great fortune. He had invested much of it there in the wild country. He loved America, and had given freely to equip the army for war. He was, therefore, a man of much influence in the campaign of the North, and no doubt those in authority there were instructed, while the war was on, to take special care of his property.

"And will you please tell me," I said at length, "who are the Misses de Lambert?"

"Daughters of a friend in Paris," said the count. "He is a great physician. He wishes not for them to marry until they are twenty-one. Mon Dieu! it was a matter of some difficulty. They were beautiful."

"Very beautiful!" I echoed.

"They were admired," he went on. "The young men they began to make trouble. My friend he send them here, with the baroness, to study — to finish their education. It is healthy, it is quiet, and — well, there are no young gentlemen. They go to bed early; they are up at daylight; they have the horse; they have boats; they amuse themselves ver' much. But they are impatient; they long for Paris — the salon, the theatre, the opera. They are like prisoners: they cannot make themselves to be contented. The baroness she has her villa on a lake back in the woods, and, mon âme! it is beautiful there — so still, so cool, so delightful! At present they have a great fear of the British. They lie awake; they listen; they expect to be carried off; they hear a sound in the night, and, mon Dieu! it is the soldiers coming."

The count laughed, lifting his shoulders with a gesture of both hands. Then he puffed thoughtfully at his cigarette.

"Indeed," he went on presently, "I think the invasion is not far away. They tell me the woods in the north are alive with British cavalry. I am not able to tell how many, but, Dieu! it is enough. The army should inform itself immediately. I think it is better that you penetrate to the river to-morrow, if you are not afraid, to see what is between, and to return by the woods. I shall trouble you to take a letter to the General Brown. It will be ready at any hour."

"At six?" I inquired.

"At six, certainly, if you desire to start then," he replied.

He rose and took my arm affectionately and conducted me to the big drawing-room. Two of the ladies were singing as one played the guitar. I looked in vain for the Misses de Lambert. The others were all there, but they had gone. I felt a singular depression at their absence and went to my room shortly to get my rest, for I had to be off early in the morning. Before going to bed, however, I sat down to think and do some writing. But I could not for the life of me put away the thought of the young ladies. They looked alike, and yet I felt sure they were very different. Somehow I could not recall in what particular they differed. I sat a time thinking over it. Suddenly I heard low voices, those of women speaking in French; I could not tell from where they came.

"I do wish she would die, the hateful thing!" said one. (It must be understood these words are more violent in English than they seem in French.)

"The colonel is severe to-night," said another.

"The colonel — a fine baroness indeed — vieille tyran! I cannot love her. Lord! I once tried to love a monkey and had better luck. The colonel keeps all the men to herself. Whom have I seen for a year? Dieu! women, grandpapas, greasy guides! Not a young man since we left Paris."

"My dear Louison!" said the other, "there are many things better than men."

"Au nom de Dieu! But I should like to know what they are. I have never seen them."

"But often men are false and evil," said the other, in a sweet, low voice.

"Nonsense!" said the first, impatiently. "I had rather elope with a one-legged hostler than always live in these woods."

"Louison! You ought to cross yourself and repeat a Hail Mary."

"Thanks! I have tried prayer. It is n't what I need. I am no nun like you. My dear sister, don't you ever long for the love of a man — a big, handsome, hearty fellow who could take

you up in his arms and squeeze the life out of
you?"

"Eh bien," said the other, with a sigh, "I
suppose it is very nice. I do not dare to think
of it."

"Nice! It is heaven, Louise! And to see a
man like that and not be permitted to — to speak
to him! Think of it! A young and handsome
man — the first I have seen for a year! Hon-
estly I could poison the colonel."

"My dear, it is the count as much as the
colonel. She is under his orders, and he has
an eagle eye."

"The old monkey! He enrages me! I
could rend him limb from limb!"

I could not help hearing what they said, but
I did not think it quite fair to share their confidence any further, so I went to one of the
windows and closed a shutter noisily. The
voices must have come from a little balcony just
under my room.

"My dear sister, you are very terrible," said
one of them, and then the shutter came to, and
I heard no more.

A full moon lighted the darkness. A little

lake gleamed like silver between the tree-tops. Worn out with hard travel, I fell into bed shortly, and lay a long time thinking of those young ladies, of the past, of to-morrow and its perils, and of the farther future. A new life had begun for me.

HE sun was lifting above the tree-tops when the count's valet called me that morning at the Château Le Ray. Robins were calling under my windows, and the groves rang with tournaments of happy song. Of that dinner-party only the count was at breakfast with me. We ate hurriedly, and when we had risen the horses were at the door. As to my own, a tall chestnut thorough-bred that Mr. Parish had brought over from England, I never saw him in finer fettle. I started Seth by Caraway Pike for Ogdensburg with the count's message.

Mine host laid hold of my elbow and gave it a good shake as I left him, with D'ri, taking a trail that led north by west in the deep woods. They had stuffed our saddle-bags with a plenty for man and horse.

I could not be done thinking of the young ladies. It put my heart in a flutter when I looked back at the castle from the wood's edge and saw one of them waving her handkerchief in a window. I lifted my hat, and put my spurs to the flank with such a pang in me I dared not look again. Save for that one thing, I never felt better. The trail was smooth, and we galloped along in silence for a mile or so. Then it narrowed to a stony path, where one had enough to do with slow going to take care of his head, there were so many boughs in the way.

"Jerushy Jane!" exclaimed D'ri, as he slowed down. "Thet air 's a gran' place. Never hed my karkiss in no sech bed as they gin me las' night — softer 'n wind, an' hed springs on like them new wagins ye see over 'n Vermont. Jerushy! Dreamed I was flyin'."

I had been thinking of what to do if we met the enemy and were hard pressed. We discussed it freely, and made up our minds that if there came any great peril of capture we would separate, each to take his own way out of the difficulty.

We halted by a small brook at midday, feeding the horses and ourselves out of the saddle-bags.

"Ain't jest eggzac'ly used t' this kind uv a sickle," said D'ri, as he felt the edge of his sabre, "but I'll be dummed ef it don't seem es ef I'd orter be ruther dang'rous with thet air 'n my hand."

He knew a little about rough fighting with a sabre. He had seen my father and me go at each other hammer and tongs there in our door-yard every day of good weather. Stormy days he had always stood by in the kitchen, roaring with laughter, as the good steel rang and the house trembled. He had been slow to come to it, but had had his try with us, and had learned to take an attack without flinching. I went at him hard for a final lesson that day in the woods — a great folly, I was soon to know. We got warm and made more noise than I had any thought of. My horse took alarm and pulled away, running into a thicket. I turned to catch him.

"Judas Priest!" said D'ri.

There, within ten feet of us, I saw what made

me, ever after, a more prudent man. It was an
English officer leaning on his sword, a tall and
handsome fellow of some forty years, in shiny
top-boots and scarlet blouse and gauntlets of
brown kid.

"You are quite clever," said he, touching his
gray mustache.

I made no answer, but stood pulling myself
together.

"You will learn," he added, smiling, with a
tone of encouragement. "Let me show you a
trick."

He was most polite in his manner, like a
play-hero, and came toward me as he spoke.
Then I saw four other Britishers coming out to
close in upon us from behind trees.

He came at me quickly, and I met him. He
seemed to think it would be no trick to unhand
my weapon. Like a flash, with a whip of his
sabre, he tried to wrench it away. D'ri had
begun to shoot, dodging between trees, and a
redcoat had tumbled over. I bore in upon my
man, but he came back at me with surprising
vigor. On my word, he was the quickest
swordsman I ever had the honor of facing.

But he had a mean way of saying "Ha!" as
he turned my point. He soon angered me,
whereupon I lost a bit of caution, with some
blood, for he was at me like a flash, and grazed
me on the hip before I could get my head again.
It was no parlor play, I can tell you. We were
fighting for life, and both knew it. We fought
up and down through brakes and bushes and
over stones — a perilous footing. I could feel
his hand weakening. I put all my speed to the
steel then, knowing well that, barring accident,
I should win. I could hear somebody coming
up behind me.

"Keep away there," my adversary shouted,
with a fairness I admire when I think of it.
"I can handle him. Get the other fellow."

I went at him to make an end of it.

"I'll make you squint, you young cub," he
hissed, lunging at me.

He ripped my blouse at the shoulder, and,
gods of war! we made the sparks fly. Then
he went down, wriggling; I had caught him in
the side, poor fellow! Like a flash I was off in
a thicket. One of the enemy got out of my
way and sent a bullet after me. I could feel it

rip and sting in the muscle as it rubbed my
ribs. I kept foot and made for my horse. He
had caught his reins, and I was on him and off
in the bush, between bullets that came ripping
the leaves about me, before they could give
chase.

Drums were beating the call to arms somewhere. I struck the trail in a minute, and,
leaning low in the saddle, went bounding over
logs and rocks and down a steep hillside as if
the devil were after me. I looked back, and
was nearly raked off by a bough. I could hear
horses coming in the trail behind with quick
and heavy jumps. But I was up to rough
riding and had little fear they would get a sight
of me. However, crossing a long stretch of
burnt timber, they must have seen me. I heard
a crack of pistols far behind; a whiz of bullets
over my head. I shook out the reins and let
the horse go, urging with cluck and spur, never
slacking for rock or hill or swale. It was a
wilder ride than any I have known since or
shall again, I can promise you, for, God knows,
I have been hurt too often. Fast riding over a
new trail is leaping in the dark and worse than

treason to one's self. Add to it a saddle wet
with your own blood, then you have something
to give you a turn of the stomach thinking
of it.

When I was near tumbling with a kind of
rib-ache and could hear no pursuer, I pulled
up. There was silence about me, save the
sound of a light breeze in the tree-tops. I
rolled off my horse, and hooked my elbow in
the reins, and lay on my belly, grunting with
pain. I felt better, having got my breath, and
a rod of beech to bite upon — a good thing if
one has been badly stung and has a journey to
make. In five minutes I was up and off at a
slow jog, for I knew I was near safety.

I thought much of poor D'ri and how he
might be faring. The last I had seen of him,
he was making good use of pistol and legs, running from tree to tree. He was a dead shot,
little given to wasting lead. The drums were
what worried me, for they indicated a big camp,
and unless he got to the stirrups in short order,
he must have been taken by overwhelming odds.
It was near sundown when I came to a brook
and falls I could not remember passing. I

looked about me. Somewhere I had gone off the old trail — everything was new to me. It widened, as I rode on, up a steep hill. Where the tree-tops opened, the hill was covered with mossy turf, and there were fragrant ferns on each side of me. The ground was clear of brush and dead timber. Suddenly I heard a voice singing — a sweet girl voice that thrilled me, I do not know why, save that I always longed for the touch of a woman if badly hurt. But then I have felt that way having the pain of neither lead nor steel. The voice rang in the silent woods, but I could see no one nor any sign of human habitation. Shortly I came out upon a smooth roadway carpeted with sawdust. It led through a grove, and following it, I came suddenly upon a big green mansion among the trees, with Doric pillars and a great portico where hammocks hung with soft cushions in them, and easy-chairs of old mahogany stood empty. I have said as little as possible of my aching wound : I have always thought it bad enough for one to suffer his own pain. But I must say I was never so tried to keep my head above me as when I came to that door. Two figures in white came out to meet me. At first I did not observe — I had enough to do keeping my eyes open — that they were the Mlles. de Lambert.

"God save us!" I heard one of them say. "He is hurt; he is pale. See the blood running off his boot-leg."

Then, as one took the bit, the other eased me down from my saddle, calling loudly for help. She took her handkerchief — that had a perfume I have not yet forgotten — as she supported me, and wiped the sweat and dust from my face. Then I saw they were the splendid young ladies I had seen at the count's table. The discovery put new life in me; it was like a dash of water in the face. I lifted my hat and bowed to them.

"Ladies, my thanks to you," I said in as good French as I knew. "I have been shot. May I ask you to send for a doctor?"

A butler ran down the steps; a gardener and a stable-boy hurried out of the grove.

"To the big room — the Louis-Quinze," said one of the girls, excitedly, as the men came to my help.

The fat butler went puffing upstairs, and they followed, on each side of me.

"Go for a doctor, quick," said one of them to the gardener, who was coming behind — a Frenchman who prayed to a saint as he saw my blood.

They led me across a great green rug in a large hall above-stairs to a chamber of which I saw little then save its size and the wealth of its appointments. The young ladies set me down, bidding one to take off my boots, and sending another for hot water. They asked me where I was hurt. Then they took off my blouse and waistcoat.

"Mon Dieu!" said one to the other. "What can we do? Shall we cut the shirt?"

"Certainly. Cut the shirt," said the other. "We must help him. We cannot let him die."

"God forbid!" was the answer. "See the blood. Poor fellow! It is terrible!"

They spoke very tenderly as they cut my shirt with scissors, and bared my back, and washed my wound with warm water. I never felt a touch so caressing as that of their light fingers, but, gods of war! it did hurt me. The bathing done, they bound me big with bandages and left the room until the butler had helped me into bed. They came soon with spirits and bathed my face and hands. One leaned over me, whispering, and asking what I would like to eat. Directly a team of horses came prancing to the door.

"The colonel!" one of them whispered, listening.

"The colonel, upon my soul!" said the other, that sprightly Louison, as she tiptoed to the window. They used to call her "Tiptoes" at the Hermitage.

The colonel! I remembered she was none other than the Baroness de Ferré; and thinking of her and of the grateful feeling of the sheets of soft linen, I fell asleep.

HE doctor came that night, and took out of my back a piece of flattened lead. It had gone under the flesh, quite half round my body, next to the ribs, without doing worse than to rake the bone here and there and weaken me with a loss of blood. I woke awhile before he came. The baroness and the fat butler were sitting beside me. She was a big, stout woman of some forty years, with dark hair and gray eyes, and teeth of remarkable whiteness and symmetry. That evening, I remember, she was in full dress.

"My poor boy!" said she, in English and in a sympathetic tone, as she bent over me.

Indeed, my own mother could not have been kinder than that good woman. She was one that had a heart and a hand for the sick-room. I told her how I had been hurt and of my ride. She heard me through with a glow in her eyes.

"What a story!" said she. "What a dare-devil! I do not see how it has been possible for you to live."

She spoke to me always in English of quaint wording and quainter accent. She seemed not to know that I could speak French.

An impressive French tutor — a fine old fellow, obsequious and bald-headed — sat by me all night to give me medicine. In the morning I felt as if I had a new heart in me, and was planning to mount my horse. I thought I ought to go on about my business, but I fear I thought more of the young ladies and the possibility of my seeing them again. The baroness came in after I had a bite to eat. I told her I felt able to ride.

"You are not able, my child. You cannot ride the horse now," said she, feeling my brow; "maybe not for a ver' long time. I have a large house, plenty servant, plenty food. Parbleu! be content. We shall take good care of you. If there is one message to go to your chief, you know I shall send it."

I wrote a brief report of my adventure with the British, locating the scene as carefully as might be, and she sent it by mounted messenger to "the Burg."

"The young ladies they wish to see you," said the baroness. "They are kind-hearted; they would like to do what they can. But I tell them no; they will make you to be very tired."

"On the contrary, it will rest me. Let them come," I said.

"But I warn you," said she, lifting her finger as she left the room, "do not fall in love. They are full of mischief. They do not study. They do not care. You know they make much fun all day."

The young ladies came in presently. They wore gray gowns admirably fitted to their fine figures. They brought big bouquets and set them, with a handsome courtesy, on the table beside me. They took chairs and sat solemn-faced, without a word, as if it were a Quaker meeting they had come to. I never saw better models of sympathetic propriety. I was about to speak. One of them shook her head, a finger on her lips.

" Do not say one word," she said solemnly in English. " It will make you ver' sick."

It was the first effort of either of them to address me in English. As I soon knew, the warning had exhausted her vocabulary. The baroness went below in a moment. Then the one who had spoken came over and sat near me, smiling.

" She does not know you can speak French," said she, whispering and addressing me in her native tongue, as the other tiptoed to the door. " On your life, do not let her know. She will never permit us to see you. She will keep us under lock and key. She knows we cannot speak English, so she thinks we cannot talk with you. It is a great lark. Are you better?"

What was I to do under orders from such authority? As they bade me, I hope you will say, for that is what I did. I had no easy conscience about it, I must own. Day after day I took my part in the little comedy. They came in Quaker-faced if the baroness were at hand, never speaking, except to her, until she had gone. Then — well, such animation, such wit, such bright eyes, such brilliancy, I have never seen or heard.

My wound was healing. War and stern duty were as things of the far past. The grand passion had hold of me. I tried to fight it down, to shake it off, but somehow it had the claws of a tiger. There was an odd thing about it all: I could not for the life of me tell which of the two charming girls I loved the better. It may seem incredible; I could not understand it myself. They looked alike, and yet they were quite different. Louison was a year older and of stouter build. She had more animation also, and always a quicker and perhaps a brighter answer. The other had a face more serious, albeit no less beautiful, and a slower tongue. She had little to say, but her silence had much in it to admire, and, indeed, to remember. They appealed to different men in me with equal force, I did not then know why. A perplexing problem it was, and I had to think and suffer much before I saw the end of it, and really came to know what love is and what it is not.

Shortly I was near the end of this delightful season of illness. I had been out of bed a week. The baroness had read to me every day, and had been so kind that I felt a great shame for

"*I could not for the life of me tell which of the
two charming girls I loved the better.*"

my part in our deception. Every afternoon she was off in a boat or in her calèche, and had promised to take me with her as soon as I was able to go.

"You know," said she, "I am going to make you to stay here a full month. I have the consent of the general."

I had begun to move about a little and enjoy the splendor of that forest home. There were, indeed, many rare and priceless things in it that came out of her château in France. She had some curious old clocks, tokens of ancestral taste and friendship. There was one her grandfather had got from the land of Louis XIV — *le Grand Monarque*, of whom my mother had begun to tell me as soon as I could hear with understanding. Another came from the bedchamber of Philip II of Spain — a grand high clock that had tolled the hours in that great hall beyond my door. A little thing, in a case of carved ivory, that ticked on a table near my bed, Molière had given to one of her ancestors, and there were many others of equal interest.

Her walls were adorned with art treasures of the value of which I had little appreciation those days. But I remember there were canvases of Correggio and Rembrandt and Sir Joshua Reynolds. She was, indeed, a woman of fine taste, who had brought her best to America; for no one had a doubt, in the time of which I am writing, that the settlement of the Compagnie de New York would grow into a great colony, with towns and cities and fine roadways, and the full complement of high living. She had built the Hermitage, — that was the name of the mansion, — fine and splendid as it was, for a mere temporary shelter pending the arrival of those better days.

She had a curious fad, this hermit baroness of the big woods. She loved nature and was a naturalist of no poor attainments. Wasps and hornets were the special study of this remarkable woman. There were at least a score of their nests on her front portico — big and little, and some of them oddly shaped. She hunted them in wood and field. When she found a nest she had it moved carefully after nightfall, under a bit of netting, and fastened somewhere about the gables. Around the Hermitage there were many withered boughs and briers holding cones

of wrought fibre, each a citadel of these uni-
formed soldiers of the air and the poisoned
arrow. They were assembled in colonies of
yellow, white, blue, and black wasps, and white-
faced hornets. She had no fear of them, and,
indeed, no one of the household was ever stung
to my knowledge. I have seen her stand in
front of her door and feed them out of a saucer.
There were special favorites that would light
upon her palm, overrunning its pink hollow and
gorging at the honey-drop.

"They will never sting," she would say, "if
one does not declare the war. To strike, to make
any quick motion, it gives them anger. Then,
mon cher ami! it is terrible. They cause you
to burn, to ache, to make a great noise, and
even to lie down upon the ground. If people
come to see me, if I get a new servant, I say :
'Make to them no attention, and they will not
harm you.'"

In the house I have seen her catch one by
the wings on a window and, holding it carefully
ask me to watch her captive — sometimes a
great daredevil hornet, lion-maned — as he lay
stabbing with his poison-dagger.

"Now," said she, "he is angry; he will remember. If I release him he will sting me when I come near him again. So I do not permit him to live — I kill him."

Then she would impale him and invite me to look at him with the microscope.

One day the baroness went away to town with the young ladies. I was quite alone with the servants. Father Joulin of the château came over and sat awhile with me, and told me how he had escaped the Parisian mob, a night in the Reign of Terror. Late in the afternoon I walked awhile in the grove with him. When he left I went slowly down the trail over which I had ridden. My strength was coming fast. I felt like an idle man, shirking the saddle, when I should be serving my country. I must to my horse and make an end to dallying. With thoughts like these for company, I went farther than I intended. Returning over the bushy trail I came suddenly upon — Louison! She was neatly gowned in pink and white.

"Le diable!" said she. "You surprise me. I thought you went another way."

"Or you would not have taken this one," I said.

"Of course not," said she. "One does not wish to find men if she is hunting for — for — " she hesitated a moment, blushing — "mon Dieu! for bears," she added.

I thought then, as her beautiful eyes looked up at me smiling, that she was incomparable, that I loved her above all others — I felt sure of it.

"And why do you hunt bears?" I inquired.

"I do not know. I think it is because they are so — so beautiful, so amiable!" she answered.

"And such good companions."

"Yes; they never embarrass you," she went on. "You never feel at loss for a word."

"I fear you do not know bears."

"Dieu! better than men. Voilà!" she exclaimed, touching me with the end of her parasol. "You are not so terrible. I do not think you would bite."

"No; I have never bitten anything but — but bread and doughnuts, or something of that sort."

"Come, I desire to intimidate you. Won't you please be afraid of me? Indeed, I can be very terrible. See! I have sharp teeth."

She turned with a playful growl, and parting
her crimson lips, showed them to me — white
and shapely, and as even as if they had been
wrought of ivory.   She knew they were beautiful, the vixen.

"You terrify me.   I have a mind to run," I
said, backing off.

"Please do not run," she answered quickly.
" I should be afraid that — that — "

She hesitated a moment, stirring the moss
with one dainty foot.

"That you might not return," she added,
smiling as she looked up at me.

"Then — then perhaps it will do as well if I
climb a tree."

"No, no ; I wish to talk with you."

"Ma'm'selle, you honor me," I said.

"And dishonor myself, I presume, with so
much boldness," she went on.   "It is only that
I have something to say ; and you know when
a woman has something to — to say — "

"It is a fool that does not listen if she be as
fair as you," I put in.

"You are — well, I shall not say what I think
of you, for fear — for fear of giving offence,"

said she, blushing as she spoke. "Do you like the life of a soldier?"

"Very much, and especially when I am wounded, with such excellent care and company."

"But your side — it was so horribly torn. I did feel very sorry — indeed I did. You will go again to the war?"

"Unless — unless — Ah, yes, ma'm'selle, I shall go again to the war," I stammered, going to the brink of confession, only to back away from it, as the blood came hot to my cheeks.

She broke a tiny bough and began stripping its leaves.

"Tell me, do you love the baroness?" she inquired as she whipped a swaying bush of brier.

The question amazed me. I laughed nervously.

"I respect, I admire the good woman — she would make an excellent mother," was my answer.

"Well spoken!" she said, clapping her hands. "I thought you were a fool. I did not know whether you were to blame or — or the Creator."

"Or the baroness," I added, laughing.

"Well," said she, with a pretty shrug, "is there not a man for every woman? The baroness she thinks she is irresistible. She has money. She would like to buy you for a plaything — to marry you. But I say beware. She is more terrible than the keeper of the Bastile. And you — you are too young!"

"My dear girl," said I, in a voice of pleading, "it is terrible. Save me! Save me, I pray you!"

"Pooh! I do not care!" — with a gesture of indifference. "I am trying to save myself, that is all."

"From what?"

"Another relative. Parbleu! I have enough." She stamped her foot impatiently as she spoke. "I should be very terrible to you. I should say the meanest things. I should call you grandpapa and give you a new cane every Christmas."

"And if you gave me also a smile, I should be content."

More than once I was near declaring myself that day, but I had a mighty fear she was play-

ing with me, and held my tongue. There was
an odd light in her eyes. I knew not, then,
what it meant.

"You are easily satisfied," was her answer.

"I am to leave soon," I said. "May I not
see you here to-morrow?"

"Alas! I do not think you can," was her
answer.

"And why not?"

"Because it would not be proper," said she,
smiling as she looked up at me.

"Not proper! I should like to know why."

"It would make me break another engage-
ment," she went on, laughing. "I am to go
with the baroness to meet the count if he comes
— she has commanded. The day after, in the
morning, at ten o'clock, by the cascade — will
that do? Good! I must leave you now. I
must not return with you. Remember!" she
commanded, pointing at me with her tapered
forefinger. "Remember — ten o'clock in the
morning."

Then she took a bypath and went out of sight.
I returned to the mansion as deep in love as a
man could be. I went to dinner with the rest

that evening. Louison came in after we were all seated.

"You are late, my dear," said the baroness.

"Yes; I went away walking and lost something, and was not able to find it again."

EXT morning the baroness went away in her glittering calèche with Louison.   Each shining spoke and golden turret flashed the sunlight back at me as I looked after them at the edge of the wood. The baroness had asked me to go with her, but I thought the journey too long. Louise came out and sat by me awhile as I lay in the hammock. She was all in white. A trifle taller and a bit more slender than her sister, I have sometimes thought her beauty was statelier, also, and more statuesque. The sight of her seemed to kindle in me the spirit of old chivalry. I would have fought and died for her with my best lance and plume. In all my life I had not seen a woman of sweeter graces of speech and manner, and, in truth, I have met some of the best born of her sex.

She had callers presently — the Sieur Michel and his daughter. I went away, then, for a walk, and, after a time, strolled into the north trail. Crossing a mossy glade, in a circle of fragrant cedar, I sat down to rest. The sound of falling water came to my ear through thickets of hazel and shadberry. Suddenly I heard a sweet voice singing a love-song of Provence — the same voice, the same song, I had heard the day I came half fainting on my horse. Somebody was coming near. In a moment I saw Louise before me.

"What, ma'm'selle!" I said; "alone in the woods!"

"Not so," said she. "I knew you were here — somewhere, and — and — well, I thought you might be lonely."

"You are a good angel," I said, "always trying to make others happy."

"Eh bien," said she, sitting beside me, "I was lonely myself. I cannot read or study. I have neglected my lessons; I have insulted the tutor — threw my book at him, and walked away, for he sputtered at me. I do not know what is the matter. I know I am very

Louise.

wicked. Perhaps — ah me! perhaps it is the devil."

"Ma'm'selle, it is appalling!" I said. "You may have injured the poor man. You must be very bad. Let me see your palm."

I held her dainty fingers in mine, that were still hard and brown, peering into the pink hollow of her hand. She looked up curiously.

"A quick temper and a heart of gold," I said. "If the devil has it, he is lucky, and — well, I should like to be in his confidence."

"Ah, m'sieur," said she, seriously, a little tremor on her lips, "I have much trouble — you do not know. I have to fight with myself."

"You have, then, a formidable enemy," I answered.

"But I am not quarrelsome," said she, thoughtfully. "I am only weary of the life here. I should like to go away and be of some use in the world. I suppose it is wicked, for my papa wishes me to stay. And bah! it is a prison — a Hôpital de Salpêtrière!"

"Ma'm'selle," I exclaimed, "if you talk like that I shall take you on my horse and fly with you. I shall come as your knight, as your deliverer, some day."

"Alas!" said she, with a sigh, "you would find me very heavy. One has nothing to do here but grow lazy and — ciel! — fat."

If my meeting with her sister had not made it impossible and absurd, I should have offered my heart to this fair young lady then and there. Now I could not make it seem the part of honor and decency. I could not help adoring her simplicity, her frankness, her beautiful form and face.

"It is no prison for me," I said. "I do not long for deliverance. I cannot tell you how happy I have been to stay — how unhappy I shall be to leave."

"Captain," she said quickly, "you are not strong; you are no soldier yet."

"Yes; I must be off to the wars."

"And that suggests an idea," said she, thoughtfully, her chin upon her hand.

"Which is?"

"That my wealth is ill fortune," she went on, with a sigh. "Men and women are fighting and toiling and bleeding and dying to make the world better, and I — I am just a lady, fussing, primping, peering into a looking-glass ! I should like to do something, but they think I am too good — too holy."

"But it is a hard business — the labors and quarrels of the great world," I suggested.

"Well — it is God's business," she continued. "And am I not one of his children, and 'wist ye not that I must be about my Father's business?' It was not too good for the man who said that."

"But what would you do ? "

"I do not know. I suppose I can do nothing because — alas ! because my father has bought my obedience with a million francs. Do you not see that I am in bondage?"

"Be patient; the life of a rich demoiselle is not barren of opportunity."

"To be gay — oh! one might as well be a peacock; to say pretty things, one might better be a well-trained parrot; to grace the court or the salon, I had as soon be a statue in the corner — it has more comfort, more security; to be admired, to hear fine compliments — well, you know that is the part of a pet poodle. I say, captain, to be happy one must be free to do."

I looked into her big eyes, that were full of their new discovery.

"I should like to be among the wounded soldiers," said she, her face brightening. "It did make me very happy to sit by your bedside and do for you."

There was a very tender look in her eyes then.

She started to rise. A brier, stirring in the breeze, had fallen across her hair. She let me loose the thorns, and, doing so, I kissed her forehead — I could not help it.

"M'sieur!" she exclaimed in a whisper. Then she turned quickly away and stood tearing a leaf in her fingers.

"Forgive me!" I pleaded, for I saw she was crying. "It was the impulse of a moment. Pray forgive me!"

She stood motionless and made no answer. I never felt such a stir in me, for I had a fear, a terrible fear, that I had lost what I might never have again.

"It was honorable admiration," I continued,

rising to my full height beside her. "Tell me, ma'm'selle, have I hurt you?"

"No," said she, in a voice that trembled. "I am thinking — I am thinking of somebody else."

The words, spoken so slowly, so sweetly, seemed, nevertheless, to fly at me. "Of somebody else!" Whom could she mean? Had her sister told her? Did she know of my meeting with Louison? I was about to confess how deeply, how tenderly, I loved her. I had spoken the first word when this thought flashed upon me, and I halted. I could not go on.

"Ma'm'selle," I said, "I — I — if it is I of whom you are thinking, give me only your pity, and I can be content. Sometime, perhaps, I may deserve more. If I can be of any service to you, send for me — command me. You shall see I am not ungrateful. Ah, ma'm'selle," I continued, as I stood to my full height, and felt a mighty uplift in my heart that seemed to toss the words out of me, "I have a strong arm and a good sword, and the love of honor and fair women."

She wiped her eyes, and turned and looked up at me. I was no longer a sick soldier.

"It is like a beautiful story," she said thought-fully; "and you — you are like a knight of old. We must go home. It is long past luncheon hour. We must hurry."

She gave me her arm up the hill, and we walked without speaking.

"I am very well to-day," I remarked as we came to the road. "If you will wait here until I get to the big birch, I shall go around to see if I can beat you to the door."

"It is not necessary," said she, smiling, "and — and, m'sieur, I am not ashamed of you or of what I have done."

The baroness and Louison had not yet returned. M. Pidgeon was at luncheon with us in the big dining room, and had much to say of the mighty Napoleon and the coalition he was then fighting.

The great monsieur stayed through the after-noon, as the baroness had planned a big house-party for the night, in celebration of the count's return. My best clothes had come by messenger from the Harbor, and I could put myself in good fettle. The baroness and the count and Louison came early, and we sat long together under the trees.

The dinner was at seven. There were more than a dozen guests, among whom were a number I had seen at the château — Mr. David Parish of Ogdensburg, who arrived late in a big, two-wheeled cart drawn by four horses that came galloping to the door, and General Wilkinson, our new commander in the North, a stout, smooth-faced man, who came with Mr. Parish in citizen's dress.

At dinner the count had much to say of scenes of excitement in Albany, where he had lately been. The baroness and her wards were resplendent in old lace and sparkling jewels. Great haunches of venison were served from a long sideboard; there was a free flow of old Madeira and Burgundy and champagne and cognac. Mr. Parish and the count and the general and Moss Kent and M. Pidgeon sat long at the table, with cigars and coffee, after the rest of us had gone to the parlors, and the big room rang with their laughter. The young Marquis de Gonvello and Mr. Marc Isambert Brunel of the Compagnie, who afterward founded the great machine-shops of the Royal Navy Yard at Portsmouth and became engineer of the Thames tunnel, and Pierre Chassinis, Jr., and I waltzed with the ladies. Presently I sat down near the baroness, who was talking in French with Thérèse Le Ray, the count's daughter.

"Pardon my using French," said the baroness, turning to me, "for I believe you do not use it, and, my friend, it is a misfortune, for you miss knowing what good company is the Ma'm'selle Le Ray."

"And I miss much pleasure and mayhap a duel with the marquis," I said, laughing; "but I beg you to proceed with your talk. I have learned many words since I came here, and I love the sound of it."

"We saw British soldiers to-day," she continued to Ma'm'selle Le Ray, in French. "They crossed the road near us on their horses."

Louison came over and sat by them.

"They were not in uniform," the baroness continued, "but I knew they were English; you cannot mistake them."

"And what do you think?" said Louison, eagerly. "One of them threatened to kiss me."

"Indeed, that was terrible," said Ma'm'selle Le Ray. "You must have been afraid."

"Yes," said she, smiling, "afraid he would n't. They were a good-looking lot."

"I do not think he was speaking of you at all," said the baroness. "He was looking at me when —"

"Ciel!" exclaimed Louison, laughing. "That is why they turned suddenly and fled into the fields."

I fled, too, — perhaps as suddenly as the Britishers, — to save myself the disgrace of laughter.

The great clock in the hall above-stairs tolled the hour of two. The ladies had all gone to bed save the baroness. The butler had started upstairs, a candelabrum in his hand. Following him were the count and Mr. Parish, supporting the general between them. The able soldier had overrated his capacity. All had risen to go to their rooms. Of a sudden we were startled by a loud rap on the front door. A servant opened it, and immediately I heard the familiar voice of D'ri.

"Is they anybody here by the name o' Mister Bell?" he asked.

I ran to the door, and there stood D'ri, his clothes wet, his boots muddy, for it had been raining. Before he could speak I had my arms around him, and he sank to his knees in my embrace. He was breathing heavily.

"Tired out — thet's whut's the matter," he muttered, leaning over on one hand. "Come through the woods t' save yer life, I did, an' they was tight up t' me all the way."

"Poor fellow!" said the baroness, who stood at the door. "Help him in at once and give him a sip of brandy."

"Tuk me prisoner over there 'n the woods thet day," said he, sinking into a chair and leaning forward, his head on his hands. "They tuk 'n' they toted me over t' Canady, an' I tuk 'n' got away, 'n' they efter me. Killed one on 'em thet was chasin' uv me over 'n the Beaver medders on the bog trail. Hoss got t' wallerin' so he hed t' come down. Riz up out o' the grass 'n' ketched holt uv 'im 'fore he c'u'd pull a weepon. Tuk this out uv his pocket, an' I tried to git the hoss out o' the mire, but did n't hev time."

He sat erect and proudly handed me a sheet of paper. I opened it, and read as follows: —

"To Captain Elias Wilkins, *Royal Fusiliers.*

"*My dear Captain:* You will proceed at once across the river with a detail of five men mounted and three days' rations, and, if possible, capture the prisoner who escaped early this morning, making a thorough search of the woods in Jefferson County. He has information of value to the enemy, and I regard his death or capture of high and immediate importance. I am informed that the young desperado who murdered my Lord of Pickford in the forest below Clayton June 29, escaping, although badly wounded, is lying at the country-seat of the Baroness de Ferré, a Frenchwoman, at Leraysville, Jefferson County, New York. It would gratify me if you could accomplish one or both captures. With respect, I am,

"Your Obedient Servant,
"R. Sheaffer, *General Commanding.*"

"They 'll be here," said D'ri. "They 'll be here jest es sure es God — 'fore daylight, mebbe. But I can't fight er dew nothin' till I 've hed some vittles."

"You shall have supper," said the baroness, who, without delay, went to the kitchen herself with a servant to look after it. The butler brought a pair of slippers and a dry coat,

while I drew off the boots of my good friend.
Then I gave him my arm as he limped to the
kitchen beside me. The baroness and I sat
near him as he ate.

"Go upstairs and call the gentlemen," said
she to the butler. "Do not make any disturb-
ance, but say I should like to speak with them
in the dining room."

"Is thet air hired man o' yours a Britisher?"
D'ri inquired as soon as the butler was gone.

"He is — from Liverpool," said she.

"Thet's the hole 'n the fence," said he.
"Thet's where the goose got away."

"The goose! The geese!" said the baroness, thoughtfully. "I do not understand you."

"Went 'n' blabbed, thet's whut he done,"
said D'ri. "Mebbe wrote 'em a letter, gol-dum
his pictur'."

"Oh, I perceive! I understand," said she;
"and I send him away to-morrow."

"Neck's broke with hunger," said D'ri.
"Never threw no vittles 'n my basket with
sech a splendid taste tew 'em es these hev."

The baroness looked at him with some show
of worry.

"I beg your pardon," said she, "did you say the neck of you was broken?"

I explained the idiom.

"Ain't hed nothin' t' eat since day 'fore yistiddy," said D'ri. "Judas Priest! I 'm all et up with hunger."

With old Burgundy and biscuit and venison and hot coffee he was rapidly reviving.

"I 'm wondering where I will hide you both," said the baroness, thoughtfully.

"Hed n't orter hev no rumpus here, 'n' go t' shootin' 'n' mebbe spile yer house 'n' furnicher," said D'ri. "'T ain't decent er 't ain't nice. We 'd better mek tracks an' put a mild er tew 'twixt us 'n' here 'fore we hev any trouble. 'T ain't a-goin' t' be no Sunday School. Ef they can, they 're a-goin' t' tek us dead er 'live. Ef they ever tuk us we would n't be wuth shucks, nuther on us, efter court martial."

"I shall not permit you to go," said the baroness. "They may be here now, about the house in the dark. They would shoot you, they would stab you, they would cause you to die as you went. No, I shall permit you not to go. There are four of them? Very well; we shall fight here, we shall conquer. We have a general, a count, a millionnaire, a marquis, a lawyer, an astronomer, a scout, and," she added, patting me on the shoulder, "*le brave capitaine!* I have four guns and three pistols, and M'sieur Bell has arms also. We shall conquer. We shall make them to bite the dust."

"Guns, did ye say? Jerushy Jane! Le' 's hev 'em," said D'ri.

"What did he call me? Mon Dieu! Jerushy Jane! It is not I," said the baroness.

Again I explained the difficulty.

"Ain't very proper-spoke," said D'ri, apologetically. "Jest wan' t' say et them air guns er likely t' come handy here 'most any minute. Give us guns, 'n' we'll sock it to 'em."

"We shall sock it to them, we shall indeed," said she, hurrying out of the room. "We shall make them to run for their lives."

They were all in the dining room — the men of the party — save the general, who could not be awakened. Guns and pistols were loaded. I made a novel plan of defence that was unanimously approved. I posted a watch at every window. A little after dawn the baroness, from

behind a curtain, saw a squad of horsemen coming through the grove.

"Ici! they have come!" said she, in a loud
whisper. "There are not four; there are
many."

I took my detail of six men above-stairs.
Each had a strip of lumber we had found in
the shop, and each carefully raised a window,
waiting the signal. I knew my peril, but I was
never so cool in my life. If I had been wiser,
possibly I should have felt it the more. The
horsemen promptly deployed, covering every
side of the mansion. They stood close,
mounted, pistol and sabre ready. Suddenly
I gave the signal. Then each of us thrust out
the strip of lumber stealthily, prodding the big
drab cones on every side. Hornets and wasps,
a great swarm of them, sprang thick as seeds
from the hand of a sower. It was my part to
unhouse a colony of the long, white-faced hornets. Goaded by the ruin of their nests, they
saw the nodding heads below them, and darted
at man and horse like a flight of arrows. They
put their hot spurs into flank and face and neck.
I saw them strike and fall; they do hit hard,

those big-winged *Vespæ.* It was terrible, the
swift charge of that winged battalion of the
air. I heard howls of pain below me, and
the thunder of rushing feet. The horses were
rearing and plunging, the men striking with
their hats.

I heard D'ri shouting and laughing at his
window.

"Give 'em hell, ye little blue devils!" he
yelled; and there was all evidence that they
understood him.

Then, again, every man of us opened his window and fired a volley at the scurrying mass.

One horse, rearing and leaping on his hind
legs, came down across the back of another, and
the two fell heavily in a rolling, convulsive
heap. One, as if blinded, bumped a tree, going
over on his withers, all fours flashing in the air.
Some tore off in the thickets, as unmanageable
as the wild moose. More than half threw their
riders. Not a man of them pulled a trigger:
they were busy enough, God knows. Not one
of them could have hit the sky with any certainty. I never saw such a torrent of horse-
hair and red caps.

"Whut! Been on the back o' one o' 'em hosses?" said D'ri, telling of it a long time after. "'D ruther o' been shet up 'n a barrel with a lot o' cats 'n' rolled downhill. Good deal better fer my health, an' I'd 'a' luked more like a human bein' when I come out. Them fellers — they did n't luk fit t' 'sociate with nuthin' er nobody when we led 'em up t' the house — nut one on 'em."

Only one Britisher was brought down by our bullets, and he had been the mark of D'ri: with him a rifle was never a plaything. Five others lay writhing in the grass, bereft of horse, deserted by their comrades. The smudges were ready, and the nets. D'ri and I put on the latter and ran out, placing a smudge row on every side of the Hermitage. The winged fighters were quickly driven away. Of the helpless enemy one had staggered off in the brush; the others lay groaning, their faces lumpy and one-sided. A big sergeant had a nose of the look and diameter of a goose-egg; one carried a cheek as large and protuberant as the jowl of a porker's head; and one had ears that stuck out like a puffed bladder. They were helpless.

We disarmed them and brought them in, doing all we could for their comfort with blue clay and bruised plantain. It was hard on them, I have often thought, but it saved an ugly fight among ladies, and, no doubt, many lives. I know, if they had taken us, D'ri and I would never have got back.

I have saved myself many a time by strategy, but chose the sword always if there were an even chance. And, God knows, if one had ever a look at our bare bodies, he would see no sign of shirking on either D'ri or me.

HE shooting and shouting and the tramp of horse and man had roused everybody in the big house. Even the general came down to know what was the matter. The young ladies came, pale and frightened, but in faultless attire. I put an armed guard by the prisoners at the door, under command of D'ri. Then I had them bare the feet of the four Britishers, knowing they could not run bootless in the brush. We organized a convoy, — the general and I, — and prepared to start for the garrison. We kept the smudges going, for now and then we could hear the small thunder of hornet-wings above us. There is a mighty menace in it, I can tell you, if they are angry.

"Jerushy Jane Pepper!" said D'ri, as he sat, rifle on his knee, looking at his prisoners.

"Never thought nobody c'u'd luk s' joemighty-ful cur'us. Does mek a man humly t' hev any trouble with them air willy-come-bobs." He meant wasps.

I had had no opportunity for more than a word with the young ladies. I hoped it might come when I went in for a hasty breakfast with the baroness, the count, the general, and Mr. Parish. As we were eating, Louison came in hurriedly. She showed some agitation.

"What is the trouble, my dear?" said the baroness, in French.

"Eh bien, only this," said she: "I have dropped my ring in the brook. It is my emerald. I cannot reach it."

"Too bad! She has dropped her ring in the brook," said the baroness, in English, turning to me.

"If she will have the kindness to take me there," I said to the hostess, rising as I spoke, "I shall try to get it for her."

"M'sieur le Capitaine, you are very obliging," said she. Then, turning to Louison, she added in French: "Go with him. He will recover it for you."

It pleased and flattered me, the strategy of
this wonderful young creature. She led me,
with dainty steps, through a dewy garden walk
into the trail.

"Parbleu!" she whispered, "is it not a shame
to take you from your meat? But I could not
help it. I had to see you; there is something
I wish to say."

"A pretty girl is better than meat," I answered quickly. "I am indebted to you."

"My! but you have a ready tongue," said
she. "It is with me a pleasure to listen. You
are going away? You shall not return — perhaps?"

She was trying to look very gay and indiffer-
ent, but in her voice I could detect a note of
trouble. The flame of passion, quenched for
a little time by the return of peril and the
smoke of gunpowder, flashed up in me.

"It is this," she went on: "I may wish you
to do me a favor. May I have your address?"

"And you may command me," I said as I
gave it to her.

"Have a care!" she said, laughing. "I may
ask you to do desperate things — you may need

all your valor. The count and the baroness —
they may send us back to France."

"Which will please you," I remarked.

"Perhaps," she said quickly. "Mon Dieu!
I do not know what I want; I am a fool. Take
this. Wear it when you are gone. Not that
I care — but — it will make you remember."

She held in her fingers a flashing emerald on
a tiny circlet of gold. Before I could answer
she had laid it in my hard palm and shut my
hand upon it.

"Dieu!" she exclaimed, whispering, "I must
return — I must hurry. Remember, we did not
find the ring."

I felt a great impulse to embrace her and
confess my love. But I was not quick enough.
Before I could speak she had turned away and
was running. I called to her, but she did not
turn or seem to hear me. She and my opportunity were gone.

We stowed the prisoners in the big coach of
the baroness, behind a lively team of four.
Then my horse and one for D'ri were brought
up.

"Do not forget," said the baroness, holding

my hand, " you are always welcome in my house.
I hope, ma foi! that you will never find happiness until you return."

The young ladies came not to the step
where we were, but stood by the count waving adieux. Louison had a merry smile and
a pretty word of French for me; Louise only
a sober look that made me sad, if it did not
speak for the same feeling in her. The
count was to remain at the Hermitage, having
sent to the château for a squad of his armed
retainers. They were to defend the house,
if, by chance, the British should renew their
attack. Mr. Parish and his footman and
the general went with us, the former driving.
D'ri and I rode on behind as the coach went
off at a gallop.

He was a great whip, that man David Parish, who had built a big mansion at Ogdensburg and owned so much of the north country
those days. He was a gentleman when the
founders of the proud families of to-day were
dickering in small merchandise. Indeed, one
might look in vain for such an establishment
as his north of Virginia. This side the

Atlantic there was no stable of horses to be compared with that he had — splendid English thoroughbreds, the blood of which is now in every great family of American horses. And, my faith! he did love to put them over the road. He went tearing up hill and down at a swift gallop, and the roads were none too smooth in that early day. Before leaving home he had sent relays ahead to await his coming every fifteen miles of the journey: he always did that if he had far to go. This time he had posted them clear to the Harbor. The teams were quickly shifted; then we were off again with a crack of the whip and a toot of the long horn. He held up in the swamps, but where footing was fair, the high-mettled horses had their heads and little need of urging. We halted at an inn for a sip of something and a bite to eat.

"Parish," said the general, rising on stiffened legs, "I like your company and I like your wine, but your driving is a punishment."

D'ri was worn out with lack of sleep and rest, but he had hung doggedly to his saddle.

"How do you feel?" I asked him as we drew up on each side of the coach.

"Split t' the collar," said he, soberly, as he rested an elbow on his pommel.

We got to headquarters at five, and turned over the prisoners. We had never a warmer welcome than that of the colonel.

"I congratulate you both," he said as he brought the rum-bottle after we had made our report. "You've got more fight in you than a wolverene. Down with your rum and off to your beds, and report here at reveille. I have a tough job for you to-morrow."

I T was, indeed, tougher business than we had yet known — a dash into the enemy's country, where my poor head was in excellent demand. D'ri and I were to cross the lake with a band of raiders, a troop of forty, under my command. We were to rescue some prisoners in a lockup on the other side. They were to be shot in the morning, and our mission therefore admitted of no delay. Our horses had been put aboard a brig at midnight, and soon after the noon mess we dropped down the lake, going into a deep, wooded cove south of the Grenadier Island. There we lay waiting for nightfall. A big wind was howling over the woods at sunset, and the dark came on its wings an hour ahead of time. The night was black and the lake noisy when we got under way, bound

for a flatboat ferry. Our skipper, it turned
out, had little knowledge of those waters. He
had shortened sail, and said he was not afraid
of the weather. The wind, out of the southeast, came harder as it drove us on. Before
we knew it, the whole kit and boodle of us
were in a devil of a shakeup there in the
broad water. D'ri and I were down among
the horses and near being trampled under
in the roll. We tried to put about then, but
the great gusts of wind made us lower sail
and drop anchor in a hurry. Soon the horses
were all in a tumble and one on top of
the other. We had to jump from back to back
to save ourselves. It was no pretty business,
I can tell you, to get to the stairway. D'ri
was stripped of a boot-leg, and I was cut
in the chin by a front hoof, going ten feet or
so to the upper deck. To the man who was
never hit in the chin by a horse's hoof let me
say there is no such remedy for a proud spirit.
Bullets are much easier to put up with and
keep a civil tongue in one's head. That
lower deck was a kind of horses' hell. We had
to let them alone. They got astraddle of one

another's necks, and were cut from ear to
fetlock — those that lived, for some of them, I
could see, were being trampled to death.
How many I never knew, for suddenly we hit
a reef there in the storm and the black night.
I knew we had drifted to the north shore, and
as the sea began to wash over us it was every
man for himself. The brig went up and down
like a sledge-hammer, and at every blow her
sides were cracking and caving. She keeled
over suddenly, and was emptied of horse and
man. A big wave flung me far among the
floundering horses. My fingers caught in a
wet mane; I clung desperately between crowding flanks. Then a big wave went over us.
I hung on, coming up astride my capture.
He swam vigorously, his nose high, blowing
like a trumpet. I thought we were in for a
time of it, and had very little hope for any
landing, save in kingdom come. Every minute
I was head under in the wash, and the roaring
filled me with that mighty terror of the windfall. But, on my word, there is no captain
like a good horse in bad water. Suddenly I
felt him hit the bottom and go forward on his

knees. Then he reared up, and began to jump
in the sand. A big wave washed him down
again. .He fell on his side in a shallow, but
rose and ran wearily over a soft beach. In the
blackness around me I could see nothing.
A branch whipped me in the face, and I
ducked. I was not quick enough; it was like
fencing in the dark. A big bough hit me,
raking the withers of my horse, and I rolled
off headlong in a lot of bushes. The horse
went on, out of hearing, but I was glad enough
to lie still, for I had begun to know of my
bruises. In a few minutes I took off my boots
and emptied them, and wrung my blouse, and
lay back, cursing my ill luck.

But that year of 1813 had the kick of ill fortune in it for every mother's son of us there in
the North country. I have ever noticed that
war goes in waves of success or failure. If we
had had Brown or Scott to lead us that year,
instead of Wilkinson, I believe it had had a better history. Here was I in the enemy's country.
God knew where, or how, or when I should
come out of it. I thought of D'ri and how it
had gone with him in that hell of waters. I

knew it would be hard to drown him. We were
so near shore, if he had missed the rocks I felt
sure he would come out safely. I thought of
Louison and Louise, and wondered if ever I
should see them again. Their faces shone upon
me there in the windy darkness, and one as
brightly as the other. Afterwhiles I drew my
wet blouse over me and went asleep, shivering.

A familiar sound woke me — that of the
reveille. The sun was shining, the sky clear,
the wind had gone down. A crow sat calling
in a tree above my head. I lay in a strip of
timber, thin and narrow, on the lake shore.
Through the bushes I could see the masts of
the brig slanting out of water some rods away.
Beyond the timber was a field of corn, climbing
a side-hill that sloped off to a level, grassy plain.
Beyond the hill-top, reveille was still sounding.
A military camp was near me, and although I
made no move, my mind was up and busy as
the drumsticks over the hill. I sat as quiet as a
cat at a mouse-hole, looking down at my uniform, not, indeed, the most healthful sort of
dress for that country. All at once I caught
sight of a scarecrow in the corn. I laughed at

the odd grotesquery of the thing — an old frock-
coat and trousers of olive-green, faded and torn
and fat with straw. A stake driven through its
collar into the earth, and crowned with an
ancient, tall hat of beaver, gave it a backbone.
An idea came to me. I would rob the scarecrow
and hide my uniform. I ran out and hauled it
over, and pulled the·stuffing out of it. The coat
and trousers were made for a stouter man. I
drew on the latter, fattening my figure with
straw to fill them. That done, I quickly donned
the coat. ·Each sleeve-end fell to my finger-
tips, and its girth would have circled a flour-
barrel and buttoned with room to spare. But
with my stuffing of straw it came around me as
snug at the belt as the coat of a bear. I took
alarm as I closed the buttons. For half a minute I had heard a drum-tap coming nearer. It
was the measured *tap ! tap ! tap-tap-tap !* so
familiar to me. Now I could hear the tread of
feet coming with it back of the hill. How soon
they would heave in sight I was unable to reckon,
but I dared not run for cover. So I thrust my
scabbard deep in the soft earth, pulled down the
big beaver hat over my face, muffled my neck

with straw, stuck the stake in front of me to
steady myself, and stood stiff as any scarecrow in
Canada. Before I was done a column, scarlet-
coated, came out in the level beyond the hillside. Through a hole in the beaver I could see
them clearly. They came on, rank after rank.
They deployed, forming an open square, scarlet-
sided, on the green turf, the gap toward me.
Then came three, walking stiffly in black coats,
a squad leading them. The thing I had taken
for a white visor was a blindfold. Their heads
were bare. I could see, now, they were in
shackles, their arms behind them. They were
coming to their death — some of my unlucky
comrades. God pity them! A spy might as
well make his peace with Heaven, if he were
caught those days, and be done with hope.
Suspicion was enough to convict on either side
of the water that year. As my feet sank deeper
in the soft earth I felt as if I were going down
to my grave. The soldiers led them into the
gap, standing them close together, backs to me.
The squad drew off. The prisoners stood erect,
their faces turning up a little, as if they were
looking into the clear, blue sky. I could see

them waver as they stood waiting. The sharp-
shooters advanced, halting as they raised their
rifles. To my horror, I saw the prisoners were
directly between me and them. Great God!
was I also of that little company about to die?
But I dared not move a step. I stood still,
watching, trembling. An officer in a shining
helmet was speaking to the riflemen. His helmet seemed to jump and quiver as he moved
away. Those doomed figures began to reel and
sway as they waited. The shiny barrels lifted a
little, their muzzles pointing at them and at me.
The corn seemed to duck and tremble as it
waited the volley. A great black ball shot
across the sky in a long curve, and began to
fall. Then came the word, a flash of fire, a
cloud of smoke, a roar of rifles that made me
jump in my tracks. I heard bullets cuffing the
corn, I felt the dirt fly up and scatter over me,
but was unhurt, a rigid, motionless man of straw.
I saw my countrymen reel, their legs go limp as
rags, their bodies fall silently forward. The
soldiers stood a moment, then a squad went
after the dead with litters. Forming in fours,
they marched away as they had come, their

steps measured by that regular *rap! rap! rap-rap-rap!* of the drum. The last rank went out of sight. I moved a little and pulled the stake, and quickly stuck it again, for there were voices near. I stood waiting as stiff as a poker. Some men were running along the beach; two others were coming through the corn. They passed within a few feet of me on each side. I heard them talking with much animation. They spoke of the wreck. When they were well by me I faced about, watching them. They went away in the timber, down to a rocky point, where I knew the wreck was visible.

They were no sooner out of sight than I pulled the stake and sabre, and shoved the latter under my big coat. Then I lifted the beaver and looked about me. There was not a soul in sight. From that level plain the field ran far to a thick wood mounting over the hill. I moved cautiously that way, for I was in the path of people who would be coming to see the wreck. I got near the edge of the distant wood, and hearing a noise, halted, and stuck my stake, and drew my hands back in the sleeves, and stood like a scarecrow, peering through my hat. Near me, in the woods, I could hear a cracking of sticks and a low voice. Shortly two Irishmen stuck their heads out of a bush. My heart gave a leap in me, for I saw they were members of my troop.

"Hello, there!" I called in a loud voice.

It startled them. They turned their heads to see where the voice came from, and stood motionless. I pulled my stake and made for them on the run. I should have known better, for the sight of me would have tried the legs of the best trooper that ever sat in a saddle. As they told me afterward, it was enough to make a lion yelp.

"Holy Mother!" said one, as they broke through the bush, running for their lives. I knew not their names, but I called them as loudly as I dared. They went on, never slacking pace. It was a bad go, for I was burning for news of D'ri and the rest of them. Now I could hear some heavy animal bounding in the brush as if their running had startled him. I went back to the corn for another stand. Suddenly a horse came up near me, cropping the brush. I saw he was one off the boat, for he had bridle and saddle, a rein hanging in two strings, and was badly cut. My friend! the sight of a horse did warm me to the toes. He got a taste of the tender corn presently, and came toward me as he ate. In a moment I jumped to the saddle, and he went away leaping like a wild deer. He could not have been more frightened if I had dropped on him out of the sky. I never saw such energy in flesh and blood before. He took a mighty fright as my hand went to his withers, but the other had a grip on the pommel, and I made the stirrups. I leaned for the strings of the rein, but his neck was long, and I could not reach them. Before I knew it we were tearing over the hill at a merry pace, I can tell you. I was never so put to it for the right thing to do, but I clung on. The big hat shook down upon my collar. In all my life I never saw a hat so big. Through the break in it I could see a farm-house. In a jiffy the horse had cleared a fence, and was running, with the feet of terror, in a dusty road. I grew angry at myself as we tore along — I knew not why. It was a rage of discomfort, I fancy, for somehow, I never felt so bound and cluttered,

so up in the air and out of place in my body.
The sabre was working loose and hammering
my knee; the big hat was rubbing my nose, the
straw chafing my chin. I had something under
my arm that would sway and whack the side of
the horse every leap he made. I bore upon it
hard, as if it were the jewel of my soul. I wondered why, and what it might be. In a
moment the big hole of my hat came into con-
junction with my right eye. On my word, it
was the stake! How it came there I have
never known, but, for some reason, I held to it.
I looked neither to right nor left, but sat erect,
one hand on the hilt of my sabre, the other in
the mane of my horse, knowing full well I was
the most hideous-looking creature in the world.
If I had come to the gate of heaven I believe
St. Peter would have dropped his keys. The
straw worked up, and a great wad of it hung
under my chin like a bushy beard. I would
have given anything for a sight of myself, and
laughed to think of it, although facing a deadly
peril, as I knew. But I was young and had no
fear in me those days. Would that a man
could have his youth to his death-bed! It was

a leap in the dark, but I was ready to take my chances.

Evidently I was nearing a village. Groups of men were in the shady thoroughfare; children thronged the dooryards. There was every sign of a holiday. As we neared them I caught my sabre under my knee, and drew my hands into the long sleeves and waved them wildly, whooping like an Indian. They ran back to the fences with a start of fear. As I passed them they cheered loudly, waving their hats and roaring with laughter. An old horse, standing before an inn, broke his halter and crashed over a fence. A scared dog ran for his life in front of me, yelping as he leaped over a stone wall. Geese and turkeys flew in the air as I neared them. The people had seemed to take me for some village youth on a masquerade. We flashed into the open country before the sound of cheering had died away. On we went over a long strip of hard soil, between fields, and off in the shade of a thick forest. My horse began to tire. I tried to calm him by gentle words, but I could give him no confidence in me. He kept on, laboring hard and breathing heavily, as if I were a ton's weight. We came to another clearing and fields of corn. A little out of the woods, and near the road, was a log house white-washed from earth to eaves. By the gate my horse went down. I tumbled heavily in the road, and turning, caught him by the bits. The big hat had shot off my head; the straw had fallen away. A woman came running out of the open door. She had bare feet, a plump and cheery face.

"Tonnerre!" said she. "Qu'est ce que cela?"

"My countrywoman," said I, in French, feeling in my under-trousers for a bit of silver, and tossing it to her, "I am hungry."

"And I have no food to sell," said she, tossing it back. "You should know I am of France and not of England. Come, you shall have enough, and for no price but the eating. You have a tired horse. Take him to the stable, and I will make you a meal."

I led my horse to the stable, scraped him of lather and dirt, gave him a swallow of water, and took the same myself, for I had a mighty thirst in me. When I came in, she had eggs and potatoes and bacon over the fire, and was filling the tea-kettle.

"On my soul," said she, frankly, "you are the oddest-looking man I ever saw. Tell me, why do you carry the long club?"

I looked down. There it was under my arm. It surprised me more than anything I ever found myself doing.

"Madame, it is because I am a fool," I said as I flung it out of the door.

"It is strange," said she. "Your clothes — they are not your own; they are as if they were hung up to dry. And you have a sabre and spurs."

"Of that the less said the better," I answered, pulling out the sabre. "Unless — unless, madame, you would like me to die young."

"Mon Dieu!" she whispered. "A Yankee soldier?"

"With good French blood in him," I added, "who was never so hungry in all his life."

I went out of the door as I spoke, and shoved my sabre under the house.

"I have a daughter on the other side of the lake," said she, "married to a Yankee, and her

husband is fighting the British with the rest of
you."

"God help him!" said I.

"Amen!" said she, bringing my food to the
table. "The great Napoleon he will teach them
a lesson."

She was a widow, as she told me, living
there alone with two young daughters who were
off at a picnic in the near town. We were
talking quietly when a familiar voice brought
me standing.

"Judas Priest!" it said. D'ri stood in the
doorway, hatless and one boot missing — a
sorry figure of a man.

"Hidin' over 'n th' woods yender," he went
on as I took his hand. "See thet air brown
hoss go by. Knew 'im soon es I sot eyes on
'im — use' t' ride 'im myself. Hed an idee 't wus
you 'n the saddle — sot s' kind o' easy. But
them air joemightyful clo's! Jerushy Jane!
would n't be fit t' skin a skunk in them clo's,
would it?"

"Got 'em off a scarecrow," I said.

"'Nough t' mek a painter ketch 'is breath,
they wus."

The good woman bade him have a chair at the table, and brought more food.

"Neck 's broke with hunger, 't is sartin," said he, as he began to eat. "Hev t' light out o' here purty middlin' soon. 'T ain' no safe place t' be. 'T won' never dew fer us t' be ketched."

We ate hurriedly, and when we had finished, the good woman gave us each an outfit of apparel left by her dead husband. It was rather snug for D'ri, and gave him an odd look. She went out of doors while we were dressing. Suddenly she came back to the door.

"Go into the cellar," she whispered. "They are coming!"

FOUND the door, and D'ri flung our "duds" into the darkness that lay beyond it. Then he made down the ladder, and I after him. It was pitch-dark in the cellar — a deep, dank place with a rank odor of rotting potatoes. We groped our way to a corner, and stood listening. We heard the tramp of horses in the dooryard and the clink of spurs on the stone step.

"Ah, my good woman," said a man with a marked English accent, "have you seen any Yankees? Woods are full of them around here. No? Well, by Jove! you're a good-looking woman. Will you give me a kiss?"

He crossed the floor above us, and she was backing away.

"Come, come, don't be so shy, my pretty woman," said he, and then we could hear her struggling up and down the floor. I was climbing the ladder, in the midst of it, my face burning with anger, and D'ri was at my heels. As the door opened, I saw she had fallen. The trooper was bending to kiss her. I had him by the collar and had hauled him down before he discovered us. In a twinkling D'ri had stripped him of sword and pistol. But it was one of the most hopeless situations in all my life. Many muzzles were pointing at us through the door and window. Another hostile move from either would have ended our history then and there. I let go and stood back. The man got to his feet — a handsome soldier in the full uniform of a British captain.

"Ah, there's a fine pair!" he said coolly, whipping a leg of his trousers with his glove. "I 'll teach you better manners, my young fellow. Some o' those shipwrecked Yankees," he added, turning to his men. "If they move without an order, pin 'em up to the wall."

He picked up his hat leisurely, stepping in front of D'ri.

"Now, my obliging friend," said he, holding out his hand, "I'll trouble you for my sword and pistol."

*" He would have fought to the death then and
there if I had but given him the word."*

D'ri glanced over at me, an ugly look in his eye. He would have fought to his death then and there if I had given him the word. He was game to the core when once his blood was up, the same old D'ri.

" Don't fight," I said.

He had cocked the pistol, and stood braced, the sword in his right hand. I noticed a little quiver in the great sinews of his wrist. I expected to see that point of steel shoot, with a quick stab, into the scarlet blouse before me.

" Shoot 'n' be damned!" said D'ri. "'Fore I die ye 'll hev a hole er tew 'n thet air karkiss o' yourn. Sha'n't give up no weepon till ye 've gin me yer word ye 'll let thet air woman alone."

I expected a volley then. A very serious look came over the face of the captain. He wiped his brow with a handkerchief. I could see that he had been drinking.

" Ah, I see! You have an interest in her. Well, my man, I want no share in your treasures. I accept the condition."

Evil as was the flavor of this poor concession, D'ri made the best of it.

"She's an honest woman for all I know,"
said he, handing over the weapons. "Ain't
a-goin' t' see no ledy mishused — nut ef I can
help it."

We gave ourselves up hand and foot to the
enemy; there was no way out of it. I have
read in the story-books how men of great nerve
and skill have slaughtered five to one, escaping
with no great loss of blood. Well, of a brave
man I like to believe good things. My own
eyes have seen what has made me slow to
doubt a story of prowess that has even the
merit of possibility. But when there are only
two of you, and one without arms, and you are
in a corner, and there are ten pistols pointing
at you a few feet away, and as many sabres
ready to be drawn, I say no power less remarkable than that of God or a novelist can bring
you out of your difficulty. You have your choice
of two evils — surrender or be cut to pieces.
We had neither of us any longing to be slashed
with steel and bored with bullets, and to no
end but a good epitaph.

They searched the cellar and found our
clothes, and wrapped them in a bundle. Then

they tied our hands behind us and took us along the road on which I had lately ridden. A crowd came jeering to the highway as we passed the little village. It was my great fear that somebody would recognize either one or both of us.

Four of our men were sitting in a guard-house at the British camp. After noon mess a teamster drove up with a big wagon. Guards came and shackled us in pairs, D'ri being wrist to wrist with me. They put a chain and ball on D'ri's leg also. I wondered why, for no other was treated with like respect. Then they bundled us all into the wagon, now surrounded by impatient cavalry. They put a blindfold over the eyes of each prisoner, and went away at a lively pace. We rode a long time, as it seemed to me, and by and by I knew we had come to a city, for I could hear the passing of many wagons and the murmur of a crowd. Some were shouting, "Shoot the d—d Yankees!" and now and then a missile struck among us. There is nothing so heartless and unthinking as a crowd, the world over. I could tell presently, by the creak

of the evener and the stroke of the hoofs, that
we were climbing a long hill. We stopped
shortly; then they began helping us out.
They led us forward a few paces, the chain
rattling on a stone pavement. When we heard
the bang of an iron door behind us, they
unlocked the heavy fetter. This done, they
led us along a gravel walk and over a sounding stretch of boards, — a bridge, I have always
thought, — through another heavy door and
down a winding flight of stone steps. They
led us on through dark passages, over stone
paving, and halted us, after a long walk,
letting our eyes free. We were in black darkness. There were two guards before and two
behind us bearing candles. They unshackled
us, and opened a lattice door of heavy iron,
bidding us enter. I knew then that we were
going into a dungeon, deep under the walls
of a British fort somewhere on the frontier.
A thought stung me as D'ri and I entered
this black hole and sat upon a heap of straw.
Was this to be the end of our fighting and of us?

"You can have a candle a day," said a guard
as he blew out the one he carried, laying it,

with a tinder-box, on a shelf in the wall of rock beside me. Then they filed out, and the narrow door shut with a loud bang. We peered through at the fading flicker of the candles. They threw wavering, ghostly shadows on every wall of the dark passage, and suddenly went out of sight. We both stood listening a moment.

"Curse the luck!" I whispered presently.

"Jest as helpless es if we was hung up by the heels," said D'ri, groping his way to the straw pile. "Ain' no use gittin' wrathy."

"What'll we do?" I whispered.

"Dunno," said he; "an' when ye dunno whut t' dew, don' dew nuthin'. Jest stan' still; thet's whut I b'lieve in."

He lighted the candle, and went about, pouring its glow upon every wall and into every crack and corner of our cell — a small chamber set firm in masonry, with a ceiling so far above our heads we could see it but dimly, the candle lifted arm's-length.

"Judas Priest!" said D'ri, as he stopped the light with thumb and finger. "I'm goin' t' set here 'n th' straw luk an ol' hen 'n' ile up m' thinker 'n' set 'er goin'. One o' them kind hes t' keep 'is mouth shet er he can't never dew no thinkin'. Bymby, like es not, I 'll hev suthin' t' say et 'll 'mount t' suthin'."

We lay back on the straw in silence. I did a lot of thinking that brought me little hope. Thoughts of Louison and Louise soon led me out of prison. After a little time I went philandering in the groves of the baroness with the two incomparable young ladies. I would willingly have stood for another bullet if I could have had another month of their company. The next thought of my troubles came with the opening of the iron door. I had been sound asleep. A guard came in with water and a pot of stewed beef and potatoes.

"Thet air 's all right," said D'ri, dipping into it with a spoon.

We ate with a fine relish, the guard, a sullen, silent man with a rough voice that came out of a bristling mustache, standing by the door.

"Luk a-here," said D'ri to the guard as we finished eating, "I want t' ast you a question. Ef you hed a purty comf'table hum on t'other side, 'n' tew thousan' dollars 'n the bank, 'n' hosses 'n' ev'rything fixed fer a good time, 'n'

all uv a sudden ye found yerself 'n sech a gol-
dum dungeon es this here, what 'u'd you dew?"

The guard was fixing the wick of his candle,
and made no answer.

"Want ye t' think it all over," said D'ri.
"See ef ye can't think o' suthin' soothin' t' say.
God knows we need it."

The guard went away without answering.

"Got him thinkin'," said D'ri, as he lighted
the candle. "He can help us some, mebbe.
Would n't wonder ef he was good et cipherin'."

"If he offered to take the two thousand, I
don't see how we'd give it to him," said I.
"He would n't take our promise for it."

"Thet ain' a-goin' t' bother us any," said
D'ri. "Hed thet all figgered out long ago."

He gave me the candle and lay down, holding his ear close to the stone floor and listening.
Three times he shifted his ear from one point
to another. Then he beckoned to me.

"Jest hol' yer ear there 'n' listen," he whispered.

I gave him the candle, and with my ear to
the floor I could hear the flow of water below
us. The sound went away in the distance and

then out of hearing. After a while it came again.

"What does it mean?" I asked.

"Cipherin' a leetle over thet air," said he, as he made a long scratch on the floor with his flint. Then he rubbed his chin, looking down at it. "Hain' jest eggzac'ly med up my mind yit," he added.

We blew out the light and lay back, whispering. Then presently we heard the coming of footsteps. Two men came to the door with a candle, one being the guard we knew.

"Come, young fellow," said the latter, as he unlocked the door and beckoned to me; "they want you upstairs."

We both got to our feet.

"Not you," he growled, waving D'ri back. "Not ready fer you yet."

He laid hold of my elbow and snapped a shackle on my wrist. Then they led me out, closing the door with a bang that echoed in the far reaches of the dark alley, and tied a thick cloth over my eyes.

"Good luck!" D'ri cried out as they took me away.

"For both," I answered as cheerfully as I could.

They led me through winding passages and iron doors, with that horrible clank of the prison latch, and up flights of stone till I felt as lost as one might who falls whirling in the air from a great height. We soon came out upon a walk of gravel, where I could feel the sweet air blowing into my face. A few minutes more and we halted, where the guard, who had hold of my elbow, rang a bell. As the door swung open they led me in upon a soft carpet. Through the cloth I could see a light.

"Bring him in, bring him in!" a voice commanded impatiently — a deep, heavy voice the sound of which I have not yet forgotten. The guard was afraid of it. His hand trembled as he led me on.

"Take off the blindfold," said that voice again.

As it fell away, I found myself in a large and beautiful room. My eyes were dazzled by the light of many candles, and for a little I had to close them. I stood before two men. One sat facing me at a black table of carved oak — a man of middle age, in the uniform of a British general. Stout and handsome, with brown eyes, dark hair and mustache now half white, and nose aquiline by the least turn, he impressed me as have few men that ever crossed my path. A young man sat lounging easily in a big chair beside him, his legs crossed, his delicate fingers teasing a thin mustache. I noticed that his hands were slim and hairy. He glanced up at me as soon as I could bear the light. Then he sat looking idly at the carpet.

The silence of the room was broken only by the scratch of a quill in the hand of the general. I glanced about me. On the wall was a large painting that held my eye: there was something familiar in the face. I saw presently it was that of the officer I had fought in the woods, the one who fell before me. I turned my head; the young man was looking up at me. A smile had parted his lips. They were the lips of a rake, it seemed to me. A fine set of teeth showed between them.

"Do you know him?" he asked coolly.

"I have not the honor," was my reply.

"What is your name?" the general demanded in the deep tone I had heard before.

" Pardon me," said the young man, quietly, as if he were now weary of the matter, " I do not think it necessary."

There was a bit of silence. The general looked thoughtfully at the young man.

" If your Lordship will let me—" he went on.

" My dear sir," the other interrupted, in the same weary and lethargic manner, " I can get more reliable knowledge from other sources. Let the fellow go back."

" That will do," said the general to the guard, who then covered my eyes and led me back to prison.

Lying there in the dark, I told D'ri all I knew of my mysterious journey. My account of the young man roused him to the soul.

" Wha' kind uv a nose hed he ?" he inquired.

" Roman," I said.

" Bent in at the p'int a leetle ? "

" Yes."

" And black hair shingled short ? "

" Yes."

" An' tall, an' a kind uv a nasty, snookin', mis'able-lookin' cuss ? "

" Just about the look of him," I said.

"Judas Priest! He's one o' them sneks et tuk me when you was fightin' t' other feller over there 'n the woods."

"Looks rather bad for us," I remarked.

"Does hev a ruther squeaky luk tew it," said he. "All we got t' dew is t' keep breathin' jest es nat'ral 'n' easy es can be till we fergit how. May fool 'em fust they know."

I had a high notion, those days, of the duty of a soldier. My father had always told me there was no greater glory for anybody than that of a brave death. Somehow the feeling got to be part of me. While I had little fear of death, I dreaded to be shot like a felon. But I should be dying for my country, and that feeling seemed to light the shadows. When I fell asleep, after much worry, it was to dream of my three countrymen who had fallen to their faces there by the corn. I awoke to find the guard in our cell, and D'ri and he whispering together. He had come with our breakfast.

"All I want," D'ri was saying, "is a piece of iron, with a sharp end, half es long es yer arm."

He made no answer, that big, sullen, bull-dog man who brought our food to us. When he had gone, D'ri lay over and began laughing under his breath.

"His thinker's goin' luk a sawmill," he whispered. "Would n't wonder ef it kep' 'im awake nights. He was askin' 'bout thet air tew thousan' dollars. Ef they 'll let us alone fer three days, we 'll be out o' here. Now, you mark my word."

"How?" I inquired.

"Jest a leetle job o' slidin' downhill," he said. "There's a big drain-pipe goes under this cell — t' the river, prob'ly. He says it 's bigger 'n a barrel."

We saved our candle that day, and walked up and down, from wall to wall, for exercise. Our hopes were high when we heard footsteps, but they fell suddenly, for, as we listened, we could hear the tramp of a squad of men. They came to our cell, and took us upstairs, blindfolded as before, to a bath-room, where the uniforms, discarded the day of our capture, were waiting for us, newly pressed. Our bath over, they directed us to put them on. They gave us new hats, for our own had been lost the night of the wreck, covered our eyes, and led us through many doors and alleys into the open air. It was dark, I knew, for as we entered a carriage I could see dimly the glow of a lantern hanging over the wheel. The carriage went away swiftly on a level road. We sat knee to knee, with two men facing us, and not a word was spoken. We could hear hoofs falling, the rattle of bit and rein, the creak of saddle-leather on each side of us. We must have gone a long journey when the carriage halted. They pulled us out roughly and led us up three steps and across a deep veranda. A bell rang, a door swung open, a flood of light fell on us, filtering to our eyes. Entering, we could feel a carpet under us, and took a dozen paces or more before they bade us halt. We heard only the low-spoken order and the soft tread of our feet. There was a dead silence when they removed our fetters and unbound our eyes. We were standing in a big and sumptuous drawing-room. A company of gentlemen sat near us in arm-chairs; there were at least a score of them. Round tables of old mahogany stood near, on which were glasses and packs of cards and wine-bottles.

The young man who sat with the general and answered to "your Lordship" was approaching me, hand extended.

"Glad to see you; sit down," he said in the same quiet, languid, forceful tone I had heard before.

It was all very odd. The guards were gone; we were apparently as free as any of them.

"I shall try to make you comfortable," he remarked. A servant began filling a row of glasses. "We have here wine and wit and all the accessories, including women. I should introduce you, but I have not the honor of your acquaintance. Let it suffice to say these are my friends" (he turned to those who sat about), "and, gentlemen, these are my enemies," he added, turning to us. "Let us hope they may die happy."

"And with a fighting chance," I added, lifting the glass without tasting it.

D'ri sat, his brows lifted, his hands in his pockets, his legs crossed. He looked curiously from one to another.

"Horton," said his Lordship, as he sat down,

leaning lazily on the arm of his chair, "will you have them bring down the prisoners?"

The servant left the room. Some of the men were talking together in low tones; they were mostly good-looking and well dressed.

"Gentlemen," said his Lordship, rising suddenly, "I'm going to turn you out of here for a moment — they're a shy lot. Won't you go into the library?"

They all rose and went out of a door save one, a bald man of middle age, half tipsy, who begged of his "Ludship" the privilege of remaining.

"Sir Charles," said the young man, still lounging in his chair as he spoke, in that cold, calm tone of his, "you annoy me. Go at once!" and he went.

They covered our faces with napkins of white linen. Then we heard heavy steps, the clank of scabbards on a stairway, the feet of ladies, and the swish of their gowns. With a quick movement our faces were uncovered. I rose to my feet, for there before me stood Louison and the Baroness de Ferré, between two guards, and, behind them, Louise, her eyes covered, her

"*Come, now, my pretty prisoner; it is disagreeable, but you must forgive me.*"

beautiful head bent low. I could see that she was crying. The truth came to me in a flash of thought. They had been taken after we left; they were prisoners brought here to identify us. A like quickness of perception had apparently come to all. We four stood looking at one another with no sign of recognition. My face may have shown the surprise and horror in me, but shortly I had recovered my stony calm. The ladies were dressed finely, with the taste and care I had so much admired. Louison turned away from me with a splendid dignity and stood looking up at the wall, her hands behind her, a toe of one shoe tapping the floor impatiently. It was a picture to remember a lifetime. I could feel my pulse quicken as I looked upon her. The baroness stood, sober-faced, her eyes looking down, her fan moving slowly. His Lordship rose and came to Louise.

"Come, now, my pretty prisoner; it is disagreeable, but you must forgive me," he said.

She turned away from him, drying her eyes. Then presently their beauty shone upon me.

"Grâce au ciel!" she exclaimed, a great joy

in her eyes and voice. "It is M'sieur Bell. Sister — baroness — it is M'sieur Bell!"

I advanced to meet her, and took her hand, kissing it reverently. She covered her face, her hand upon my shoulder, and wept in silence. If it meant my death, I should die thanking God I knew, or thought I knew, that she loved me.

"Ah, yes; it is M'sieur Bell — poor fellow!" said Louison, coming quickly to me. "And you, my dear, you are Ma'm'selle Louise."

She spoke quickly in French, as if quite out of patience with the poor diplomacy of her sister.

"I knew it was you, for I saw the emerald on your finger," she added, turning to me, "but I could not tell her."

"I am glad, I am delighted, that she spoke to me," I said. I desired to save the fair girl, whose heart was ever as a child's, any sorrow for what she had done. "I was about to speak myself. It is so great a pleasure to see you all I could not lónger endure silence."

"They made us prisoners; they bring us here. Oh, m'sieur, it is terrible!" said the baroness.

"And he is such a horrible-looking mon-key!" said Louison.

"Do they treat you well?" I asked.

"We have a big room and enough to eat. It is not a bad prison, but it is one terrible place," said the baroness. "There is a big wall; we cannot go beyond it."

"And that hairy thing! He is in love with Louise. He swears he will never let us go," said Louison, in a whisper, as she came close to me, "unless — unless she will marry him."

"Ah! a tea-party," said his Lordship, com-ing toward us. "Pardon the interruption. I have promised to return these men at nine. It is now ten minutes of the hour. Ladies, I wish you all a very good night."

He bowed politely. They pressed my hand, leaving me with such anxiety in their faces that I felt it more than my own peril. Louison gave me a tender look out of her fine eyes, and the thought of it was a light to my soul in many an hour of darkness. She had seemed so cool, so nonchalant, I was surprised to feel the tremor in her nerves. I knew not words to say when Louise took my hand.

"Forgive me — good-by!" said she.

It was a faint whisper out of trembling lips.
I could see her soul in her face then. It was
lighted with trouble and a nobler beauty than
I had ever seen. It was full of tenderness and
pity and things I could not understand.

"Have courage!" I called as they went
away.

I was never in such a fierce temper as when,
after they had gone above-stairs, I could hear
one of them weeping. D'ri stood quietly beside
me, his arms folded.

"Whut ye goin' t' dew with them air women?"
he asked, turning to the young man.

"I beg you will give me time to consider,"
said his Lordship, calmly, as he lighted a
cigarette.

There was a quick move in the big tower of
bone and muscle beside me. I laid hold of
D'ri's elbow and bade him stop, or I fear his
Lordship's drawing-room, his Lordship, and
ourselves would presently have had some need
of repair. Four guards who seemed to be waiting in the hall entered hurriedly, the shackles
in hand.

"No haste," said his Lordship, more pleasantly than ever. "Stand by and wait my orders."

"D'ye wan' t' know whut I think o' you?" said D'ri, looking down at him, his eyes opening wide, his brow wrinkling into long furrows.

"I make a condition," said his Lordship: "do not flatter me."

"Yer jest a low-lived, mis'able, wuthless pup," said D'ri.

"Away with them!" said his Lordship, flicking the ashes off a cigarette as he rose and walked hurriedly out of the room.

T HE waiting guards laid hold of us in a twinkling, and others came crowding the doors. They shackled our hands behind us, and covered our eyes again. Dark misgivings of what was to come filled me, but I bore all in silence. They shoved us roughly out of doors, and there I could tell they were up to no child's play. A loud jeer burst from the mouths of many as we came staggering out. I could hear the voices of a crowd. They hurried us into a carriage.

"We demand the prisoners!" a man shouted near me.

Then I could hear them scuffling with the guards, who, I doubt not, were doing their best to hold them back. In a moment I knew the mob had possession of us and the soldiers were being hustled away. D'ri sat shoulder to

shoulder with me. I could feel his muscles
tighten ; I could hear the cracking of his joints
and the grinding of the shackle-chain. "Judas
Pr-r-i-e-st ! " he grunted, straining at the iron.
Two men leaped into the carriage. There was
a crack of the whip, and the horses went off
bounding. We could hear horsemen all about
us and wagons following. I had a stout heart
in me those days, but in all my life I had never
taken a ride so little to my liking. We went
over rough roads, up hill and down, for an hour
or more.

I could see in prospect no better destination
than our graves, and, indeed, I was not far
wrong. Well, by and by we came to a town
somewhere — God knows where. I have never
seen it, or known the name of it, or even that
of the prison where we were first immured. I
could tell it was a town by the rumble of the
wheels and each echoing hoof-beat. The cavalcade was all about us, and now and then we
could hear the sound of voices far behind. The
procession slowed up, horsemen jammed to the
left of us, the carriage halted. I could hear
footsteps on a stone pavement.

"You're late," said a low voice at the carriage door. "It's near eleven."

"Lot o' fooling with the candidates," said one of the horsemen, quietly. "Everything ready?"

"Everything ready," was the answer.

The carriage door swung open.

"We get out here," said one of the men who sat with us.

I alighted. On each side of me somebody put his hand to my shoulder. I could see the glow of a lantern-light close to my face. I knew there was a crowd of men around, but I could hear nothing save now and then a whisper.

"Wall, Ray," said D'ri, who stood by my side, "hol' stiddy 'n' don't be scairt."

"Do as they tell ye," a stranger whispered in my ear. "No matter what 't is, do as they tell ye."

They led us into a long passage and up a steep flight of wooden stairs. I have learned since then it was a building equipped by a well-known secret society for its initiations.[1] We

[1] The intrepid Fitzgibbon, the most daring leader on the Canadian frontier those days, told me long afterward that he

went on through a narrow hall and up a winding
flight that seemed to me interminable. Above
it, as we stopped, the man who was leading me
rapped thrice upon a rattling wooden door. It
broke the silence with a loud echoing noise. I
could hear then the sliding of a panel and a
faint whispering and the sound of many feet
ascending the stairs below. The door swung
open presently, and we were led in where I
could see no sign of any light. They took me
alone across a wide bare floor, where they set me
down upon some sort of platform and left me,
as I thought. Then I could hear the whispered
challenge at the door and one after another
entering and crossing the bare floor on tiptoe.
Hundreds were coming in, it seemed to me.

knew the building — a tall frame structure on the high shore of
a tributary of the St. Lawrence. It was built on a side of the
bluff and used originally as a depot for corn, oats, rye, and
potatoes, that came down the river in bateaux. The slide was
a slanting box through which the sacks of grain were conveyed
to sloops and schooners below. It did not pay and was soon
abandoned, whereupon it was rented by the secret order referred
to above. The slide bottom was coated with lard and used for
the hazing of candidates. A prize fight on the platform was
generally a feature of the entertainment. A man was severely
injured in a leap on the bayonets, after which that feature of
the initiation was said to have been abandoned.

Suddenly a deep silence fell in that dark place of evil. The blindfold went whisking off my head as if a ghostly hand had taken it. But all around me was the darkness of the pit. I could see and I could hear nothing but a faint whisper, high above me, like that of pine boughs moving softly in a light breeze. I could feel the air upon my face. I thought I must have been moved out of doors by some magic. It seemed as if I were sitting under trees alone. Out of the black silence an icy hand fell suddenly upon my brow. I flinched, feeling it move slowly downward over my shoulder. I could hear no breathing, no rustle of garments near me. In that dead silence I got a feeling that the hand touching me had no body behind it. I was beyond the reach of fear — I was in a way prepared for anything but the deep, heart-shaking horror that sank under the cold, damp touch of those fingers. They laid hold of my elbow firmly, lifting as if to indicate that I was to rise. I did so, moving forward passively as it drew me on. To my astonishment I was unable to hear my own footfall or that of my conductor. I thought we were walking upon soft earth.

Crossing our path in front of me I could see, in the darkness, a gleaming line. We moved slowly, standing still as our toes covered it. Then suddenly a light flashed from before and below us. A cold sweat came out upon me; I staggered back to strong hands that were laid upon my shoulders, forcing me to the line again. By that flash of light I could see that I was standing on the very brink of some black abyss — indeed, my toes had crossed the edge of it. The light came again, flickering and then settling into a steady glow. The opening seemed to have a grassy bottom some ten feet below. In front of me the soil bristled, on that lower level, with some black and pointed plant: there was at least a score of them. As I looked, I saw they were not plants, but a square of bayonets thrust, points up, in the ground. A curse came out of my hot mouth, and then a dozen voices mocked it, going fainter, like a dying echo. I heard a whisper in my ear. A tall figure in a winding-sheet, its face covered, was leaning over me.

"To hesitate is to die," it whispered. "Courage may save you."

Then a skeleton hand came out of the wind-ing-sheet, pointing down at the square of bris-tling bayonets. The figure put its mouth to my ear.

"Jump!" it whispered, and the bare bones of the dead fingers stirred impatiently.

Some seconds of a brief silence followed. I could hear them slowly dripping out of eternity in the tick of a watch near me. I felt the stare of many eyes invisible to me. A broad beam of bright light shot through the gloom, resting full upon my face. I started back upon the strong hands behind me. Then I felt my muscles tighten as I began to measure the fall and to wonder if I could clear the bayonets. I had no doubt I was to die shortly, and it mattered not to me how, bound as I was, so that it came soon. For a breath of silence my soul went up to the feet of God for help and hope. Then I bent my knees and leaped. I saw much as my body went rushing through the air — an empty grave its heap of earth beside it, an island of light, walled with candles, in a sea of gloom, faces showing dimly in the edge of the darkness. "Thank God! I shall clear the bayonets," I thought, and struck heavily upon a soft mat, covered over with green turf, a little beyond that bristling bed. I staggered backward, falling upon it. To my surprise, it bent beneath me. They were no bayonets, but only shells of painted paper. I got to my feet none the worse for jumping, and as dumfounded as ever a man could be. I stood on a lot of broken turf with which a wide floor had been overlaid. Boards and timbers were cut away, and the grave dug beneath them. I saw one face among others in the gloom beyond the candle rows — that of his Lordship. He was coming up a little flight of stairs to where I stood. He moved the candles, making a small passage, and came up to me.

"You're a brave man," said he, in that low, careless tone of his.

"And you a coward," was my answer, for the sight of him had made me burn with anger.

"Don't commit yourself on a point like that," said he, quickly, "for, you know, we are not well acquainted. I like your pluck, and I offer you what is given to few here — an explanation."

He paused, lighting a cigarette. I stood

looking at him. The cold politeness of manner with which he had taken my taunt, his perfect self-mastery, filled me with wonder. He was no callow youth, that man, whoever he might be. He was boring at the floor with the end of a limber cane as he continued to address me.

"Now, look here," he went on, with a little gesture of his left hand, between the fingers of which a cigarette was burning. "You are now in the temple of a patriotic society acting with no letters patent, but in the good cause of his Most Excellent Majesty King George III, to whom be health and happiness."

As he spoke the name he raised his hat, and a cheer came from all sides of us.

"It is gathered this night," he continued, "to avenge the death of Lord Ronley, a friend of his Majesty, and of many here present, and an honored member of this order. For his death you, and you alone, are responsible, and, we suspect, under circumstances of no credit to your sword. Many of our people have been cut off from their comrades and slain by cowardly stealth, have been led into ambush and cruelly cut to pieces by an overwhelming

number, have been shut in prison and done to
death by starvation or by stabs of a knife there
in your country. Not content with the weapons
of a soldier, you have even resorted to the barbarity of the poison-wasp. Pardon me, but you
Yankees do not seem to have any mercy or fairness for a foe. We shall give you better treat-
ment. You shall not be killed like a rat in a
trap. You shall have a chance for your life.
Had you halted, had you been a coward, you
would not have been worthy to fight in this
arena. You would not have come where you
are standing, and possibly even now your grave
would have been filled. If you survive the
ordeal that is to come, I hope it will prove an
example to you of the honor that is due to bravery, of the fairness due a foe."

Many voices spoke the word " Amen " as he
stopped, turning to beckon into the gloom
about us. I was now quite over my confusion.
I began to look about me and get my bearings.
I could hear a stir in the crowd beyond the
lights, and a murmur of voices. Reflecting
lanterns from many pillars near by shot their
rays upon me. I stood on a platform, some

thirty feet square, in the middle of a large room. Its floor was on a level with the faces of the many who stood pressing to the row of lights. Here, I took it, I was to fight for my life. I was looking at the yawning grave in the corner of this arena, when four men ascended with swords and pistols. One of them removed the shackles, letting my hands free. I thanked him as he tossed them aside. I was thinking of D'ri, and, shading my eyes, looked off in the gloom to see if I could discover him. I called his name, but heard no answer. His Lordship came over to me, bringing a new sword. He held the glittering blade before me, its hilt in his right hand, its point resting on the fingers of his left.

"It's good," said he, quietly; "try it."

It was a beautiful weapon, its guard and pommel and quillons sparkling with wrought-silver, its grip of yellow leather laced with blue silk. The glow and the feel of it filled me with a joy I had not known since my father gave me the sword of my childhood. It drove the despair out of me, and I was a new man. I tried the blade, its point upon my toe. It was good metal, and the grip fitted me.

"Well, how do you find it?" said he, impatiently.

"I am satisfied," was my reply.

He helped me take off my blouse and waistcoat, and then I rolled my sleeves to the elbow. The hum of voices had grown louder. I could hear men offering to bet and others bantering for odds.

"We'll know soon," said a voice near me, "whether he could have killed Ronley in a fair fight."

I turned to look at those few in the arena. There were half a dozen of them now, surrounding my adversary, a man taller than the rest, with a heavy neck and brawny arms and shoulders. He had come out of the crowd unobserved by me. He also was stripped to the shirt, and had rolled up his sleeves, and was trying the steel. He had a red, bristling mustache and overhanging brows and a vulgar face — not that of a man who settles his quarrel with the sword. I judged a club or a dagger would have been better suited to his genius. But, among fighters, it is easy to be fooled by a face. In a moment the others had gone save his Lordship and that portly bald-headed man I had heard him rebuke as " Sir Charles." My adversary met me at the centre of the arena, where we shook hands. I could see, or thought I could, that he was entering upon a business new to him, for there was in his manner an indication of unsteady nerves.

" Gentlemen, are you ready ? " said his Lordship.

But there are reasons why the story of what came after should be none of my telling. I leave it to other and better eyes that were not looking between flashes of steel, as mine were. And then one has never a fair view of his own fights.

HIS is the story of Corporal Darius Olin, touching his adventure in the Temple of the Avengers, at some unknown place in Upper Canada, on the night of August 12, 1813, and particularly the ordeals of the sword, the slide, and the bayonet to which Captain Ramon Bell was subjected that night, as told to Adjutant Asarius Church, at Sackett's Harbor, New York : —

"Soon es I see whut wus up, I gin a powerful lift on thet air shackle-chain. I felt 'er give 'n' bust. A couple o' men clim' int' the seat front uv us, 'n' the hosses started hell bent. I sot up with my hands 'hind uv me 'n the wagin. I kep' 'em there tight 'n' stiff, es ef the iron wus holdin' uv 'em. Could n't git no chance t' say nuthin' t' Ray. Hustled us upstairs, 'n' when we come in t' thet air big room they tuk him one way an' me 'nother.

"Did n't hev no idee where I wus. Felt 'em run a chain through my arms, careful, efter they sot me down. I sot still fer mebbe five minutes. Seemed so ev'rybody'd gone out o' the place. Could n't hear nuthin' nowhere. I le' down the chain jest es ca-areful 'es I could, 'n' tuk off the blindfold. 'T was all dark; could n't see my hand afore me. Crep' 'long the floor. See 't was covered with sawdust. Tuk off m' boots, 'n' got up on m' feet, 'n' walked careful. Did n' dast holler t' Ray. Cal'lated when the squabble come I'd be ready t' dew business. All t' once I felt a slant 'n the floor. 'T was kind o' slip'ry, 'n' I begun t' slide. Feet went out from under me 'n' sot me down quick. Tried t' ketch holt o' suthin'. Could n't hang on; kep' goin' faster. Fust I knew I'd slid int' some kind uv a box. Let me down quicker 'n scat over thet air grease a little ways. I out with my tew hands 'n' bore ag'in' the sides o' th' box powerful 'n' stopped myself. Then I up with these here feet o' mine. See the top o' the box wa'n't much more 'n a foot above me. Tried t' crawl up ag'in. Could n't mek it. Dum thing slanted

luk Tup's Hill. Hung on awhile, cipherin' es
hard es I knew how. Hearn suthin' go kerslap.
Seem so the hull place trembled. Raised up
my head, 'n' peeked over my stumick down the
box. A bar o' light stuck in away down. Let
myself go careful till I c'u'd see my nose in it.
Then I got over on my shoulder 'n' braced on
the sides o' the box, back 'g'in' one side 'n'
knees 'g'in' t'other. See 't was a knot-hole
where the light come in, 'bout es big es a man's
wrist. Peeked through, 'n' see a lot o' lights
'n' folks, 'n' hearn 'em talkin'. Ray he stud on
a platform facin' a big, powerful-lookin' cuss.
Hed their coats 'n' vests off, 'n' sleeves rolled
up, 'n' swords ready. See there wus goin' t' be
a fight. Hed t' snicker — wa'n' no way I c'u'd
help it, fer, Judas Priest! I knew dum well they
wa'n't a single one of them air Britishers c'u'd
stan' 'fore 'im. Thet air mis'able spindlin'
devil I tol' ye 'bout — feller et hed the women
— he stud back o' Ray. Hed his hand up luk
thet. 'Fight!' he says, 'n' they got t' work,
'n' the crowd begun t' jam up 'n' holler. The
big feller he come et Ray es ef he wus goin' t'
cut him in tew. Ray he tuk it easy 'n' rassled

the sword of the big chap round 'n' round es ef
it wus tied t' hisn. Fust I knew he med a
quick lunge 'n' pricked 'im 'n the arm. Big
chap wus a leetle shy then. Did n't come up t'
the scratch es smart 'n' sassy es he'd orter.
Ray he went efter 'im hammer 'n' tongs. Thet
air long slim waist o' hisn swayed 'n' bent luk
a stalk o' barley. He did luk joemightyful
han'some — wish 't ye c'u'd 'a' seen 'im thet air
night. Hair wus jest es shiny es gold 'n the
light o' them candles. He'd feint, an' t' other
'd dodge. Judas Priest! seemed so he put the
p'int o' the sword all over thet air big cuss.
C'u'd 'a' killed 'im a dozen times, but I see he
did n't want t' dew it. Kep' prickin' 'im ev'ry
lunge 'n' druv 'im off the boards — tumbled 'im
head over heels int' the crowd. Them air
devils threw up their hats 'n' stomped 'n' hollered powerful, es ef 't were mighty fun t' see
a man cut t' pieces. Wall, they tuk up another
man, quicker 'n the fust, but he wa'n' nowhere
near s' big 'n' cordy. Wa'n't only one crack o'
the swords in thet air fight. Could n't hardly say
Jack Robinson 'fore the cuss hed fell. Ray
hurt him bad, I guess, for they hed t' pick 'im

up 'n' carry 'im off luk a baby. Guess the boy
see 't he hed a good many to lick, 'n' hed n't
better waste no power a-foolin'. All t' once thet
air low-lived, spindlin', mis'able devil he come
t' the edge o' the platform 'n' helt up his hand.
Soon 's they stopped yellin' he says: 'Gentlemen,' he says, 'sorry t' tell ye thet the man fer
the next bout hes got away. We left him
securely fastened up 'n the fust chamber.
Have hed the building searched, but ain't able
t' find him. He must hev gone down the slide.
I am sorry to say we hev no more Yankees. If
this man fights any more it will hev t' be a
Britisher thet goes ag'in' 'im. Is there a
volunteer?'

"Ray he runs up 'n' says suthin' right 'n his
ear. Could n't hear whut 't wus. Did n' set
well. T' other feller he flew mad, 'n' Ray he
fetched 'im a cuff, luk thet, with the back uv
his hand. Ye see, he did n' know he hed been
a-fightin' Yankees, 'n' he did n' like the idee.
'Gentlemen,' says he, 'I 'll fight anybody, but ef
this chap ain't a coward, he 'll fight me himself.'
T' other feller he off with his coat 'n' vest es
quick es a flash 'n' picked up a sword. 'Fight,

then, ye cub !' says he; an' they flew at each
other hell bent fer 'lection. He wa'n' no fool
with a sword, nuther, I can tell ye, thet air
spindlin' cuss. I see Ray hed his han's full.
But he wus jest es cool es a green cowcumber,
eggzac'ly. Kep' a-cuffin' t' other sword, 'n' let
'im hit 'n' lunge 'n' feint es much es he pleased.
See he wus jest a-gettin' his measure, 'n' I knew
suthin' wus goin' t' happen purty quick. Fust
I knew he ketched Ray by the shirtsleeve with
the p'int uv 'is sword 'n' ripped it t' the collar.
Scairt me so I bit my tongue watchin' uv 'em.
They got locked, 'n' both swords came up t' the
hilts t'gether with a swish 'n' a bang luk thet.
The blades clung, 'n' they backed off. Then
Ray he begun t' feint 'n' lunge 'n' hustle 'im.
Quicker 'n scat he gin 'im an awful prick 'n the
shoulder. I c'u'd see the blood come, but they
kep' a-goin' back 'n' forth 'n' up 'n' down
desperit. The red streak on thet air feller's
shirt kep' a-growin'. Purty quick one side uv
'im wus red an' t' other white. See he wus
gettin' weaker 'n' weaker. Ray c'u'd 'a' split
'im t' the navel ef he 'd only hed a min' tew.
All t' once he med a jab at Ray, 'n' threw up

'is han's, 'n' went back a step er tew, luk a hoss
with th' blin' staggers, 'n' tumbled head over
heels in thet air open grave. There wus hell
t' pay fer a minute. Lot on 'em clim' over the
row o' lights, yellin' luk wildcats, 'n' hauled thet
air mis'able cuss out o' the grave, 'n' stud 'im
up, 'n' gin 'im a drink o' liquor. In half a
minute he up with his han'kerchief 'n' waved
it over 'is head t' mek 'em keep still. Soon 's
they wus quiet he up 'n' he says: 'Gentlemen,'
says he, 'this 'ere chap hes stood the test o' the
sword. Are ye satisfied?' 'We are,' says
they — ev'ry British son uv a gun they wus
there up 'n' hollered. 'Then,' says he, 'giv'
'im th' slide.'

"Ray he put down 'is sword 'n' picked up 'is
coat 'n' vest. Then they grabbed th' lights, 'n'
thet 's th' last I see on' em there. Purty quick
't wus all dark. Hearn 'em comin' upstairs 'n
goin' 'cross th' floor over my head. 'Gun t'
think o' myself a leetle bit then. Knowed I
was in thet air slide, an' hed t' le' go purty quick.
Hed n't no idee where it went tew, but I cal'-
lated I wus middlin' sure t' know 'fore long.
Knowed when I le' go I wus goin' t' dew some

tall slippin' over thet air greased bottom. See
a light come down th' box 'n a minute. Hearn
somebody speakin' there et the upper end.

" 'This 'ere 's th' las' test o' yer courage,' says
a man, says he; ' few comes here alive 'n' sound
es you be. Ye wus a doomed man. Ye 'd hev
been shot at daylight, but we gin ye a chance
fer yer life. So fur ye 've proved yerself wuthy.
Ef ye hold yer courage, ye may yit live. Ef
ye flinch, ye 'll land in heaven. Ef yer life is
spared, remember how we honor courage.'

" Then they gin 'im a shove, 'n' I hearn 'im
a-comin'. I flopped over 'n' le' go. Shot away
luk a streak o' lightnin'. Dum thing grew
steeper 'n' steeper. Jes' hel' up my han's 'n' let
'er go lickitty split. Jerushy Jane Pepper ! jes'
luk comin' down a greased pole. Come near
tekin' my breath away — did sart'n. Went out
o' thet air thing luk a bullet eggzac'ly. Shot
int' the air feet foremust. Purty fair slidin' up
in the air 'most anywheres, ye know. Alwus
come down by the nighest way. 'T was darker
'n pitch; could n't see a thing, nut a thing.
Hearn Ray come out o' the box 'bove me.
Then I come down k'slap in th' water 'n' sunk.

Thought I 'd never stop goin' down. 'Fore I
come up I hearn Ray rip int' th' water nigh
me. I come up 'n' shook my head, 'n' waited.
Judas Priest! thought he wus drownded, sart'n.
Seemed so I 'd bust out 'n' cry there 'n th' water
waitin' fer thet air boy. Soon es I hearn a flop
I hed my han's on 'im.

"'Who be you?' says he.

"'D'ri,' says I.

"'Tired out,' says he; 'can't swim a stroke.
Guess I 'll hev t' go t' th' bottom.'"

'RI'S narrative was the talk of the garrison. Those who heard the telling, as I did not, were fond of quoting its odd phrases, and of describing how D'ri would thrust and parry with his jack-knife in the story of the bouts.

The mystery of that plunge into darkness and invisible water was a trial to my nerves the like of which I had never suffered. After they had pulled his Lordship out of the grave, and I knew there would be no more fighting, I began to feel the strain he had put upon me. He was not so strong as D'ri, but I had never stood before a quicker man. His blade was as full of life and cunning as a cat's paw, and he tired me. When I went under water I felt sure it was all over, for I was sick and faint. I had been thinking of D'ri in that quick descent. I wondered if he was the man who had got away and gone down the slide. I was not the less amazed, however, to feel his strong hand upon me as I came up. I knew nothing for a time. D'ri has told me often how he bore me up in rapid water until he came into an eddy where he could touch bottom. There, presently, I got back my senses and stood leaning on his broad shoulder awhile. A wind was blowing, and we could hear a boat jumping in the ripples near by. We could see nothing, it was so dark, but D'ri left me, feeling his way slowly, and soon found the boat. He whistled to me, and I made my way to him. There were oars in the bottom of the boat. D'ri helped me in, where I lay back with a mighty sense of relief. Then he hauled in a rope and anchor, and shoved off. The boat, overrunning the flow in a moment, shot away rapidly. I could feel it take headway as we clove the murmuring waters. D'ri set the oars and helped it on. I lay awhile thinking of all the blood and horror in that black night — like a dream of evil that leads through dim regions of silence into the shadow of death. I thought of the hinted peril of the slide that was to be the punishment of poor courage.

D'ri had a plausible theory of the slide. He said that if we had clung to the sides of it to break our speed we'd have gone down like a plummet and shattered our bones on a rocky shore. Coming fast, our bodies leaped far into the air and fell to deep water. How long I lay there thinking, as I rested, I have no satisfactory notion. Louise and Louison came into my thoughts, and a plan of rescue. A rush of cavalry and reeking swords, a dash for the boats, with a flying horse under each fair lady, were in that moving vision. But where should we find them? for I knew not the name of that country out of which we had come by ways of darkness and peril. The old query came to me, If I had to choose between them, which should I take? There was as much of the old doubt in me as ever. For a verity, I loved them both, and would die for either. I opened my eyes at last, and, rising, my hands upon the gunwales, could dimly see the great shoulders of D'ri swaying back and forth as he rowed. The coming dawn had shot an arrow into the great,

black sphere of night, cracking it from circum-
ference to core, and floods of light shortly came
pouring in, sweeping down bridges of darkness,
gates of gloom, and massy walls of shadow.
We were in the middle of a broad river — the
St. Lawrence, we knew, albeit the shores were
unfamiliar to either of us. The sunlight stuck
in the ripples, and the breeze fanned them into
flowing fire. The morning lighted the green
hills of my native land with a mighty splendor.
A new life and a great joy came to me as I filled
my lungs with the sweet air. D'ri pulled into
a cove, and neither could speak for a little. He
turned, looking out upon the river, and brushed
a tear off his brown cheek.

"No use talkin'," said he, in a low tone, as
the bow hit the shore, "ain' no country luk this
'un, don' care where ye go."

As the oars lay still, we could hear in the far
timber a call of fife and drum. Listening, we
heard the faint familiar strains of "Yankee
Doodle." We came ashore in silence, and I
hugged the nearest tree, and was not able to say
the "Thank God!" that fell from my lips only
half spoken.

E got our bearings, a pair of boots for D'ri, and a hearty meal in the cabin of a settler. The good man was unfamiliar with the upper shore, and we got no help in our mystery. Starting west, in the woods, on our way to the Harbor, we stopped here and there to listen, but heard only wood-thrush and partridge — the fife and drum of nature. That other music had gone out of hearing. We had no compass, but D'ri knew the forest as a crow knows the air. He knew the language of the trees and the brooks. The feel of the bark and what he called "the lean of the timber" told him which way was south. River and stream had a way of telling him whence they had come and where they were going, but he had no understanding of a map. I remember, after we had come to the Harbor at dusk and told our story, the general asked him to indicate our landing-place and our journey home on a big map at headquarters. D'ri studied the map a brief while. There was a look of embarrassment on his sober face.

"Seems so we come ashore 'bout here," said he, dropping the middle finger of his right hand in the vicinity of Quebec. "Then we travelled aw-a-a-ay hellwards over 'n this 'ere direction." With that illuminating remark he had slid his finger over some two hundred leagues of country from Quebec to Michigan.

They met us with honest joy and no little surprise that evening as we came into camp. Ten of our comrades had returned, but as for ourselves, they thought us in for a long stay. We said little of what we had gone through, outside the small office at headquarters, but somehow it began to travel, passing quickly from mouth to mouth, until it got to the newspapers and began to stir the tongue of each raw recruit. General Brown was there that evening, and had for me, as always, the warm heart of a father. He heard our report with a kindly sympathy.

Next morning I rode away to see the Comte de Chaumont at Leraysville. I had my life, and a great reason to be thankful, but there were lives dearer than my own to me, and they were yet in peril. Those dear faces haunted me and filled my sleep with trouble. I rode fast, reaching the château at luncheon time. The count was reading in a rustic chair at the big gate. He came running to me, his face red with excitement.

"M'sieur le Capitaine!" he cried, my hand in both of his, "I thought you were dead."

"And so I have been — dead as a cat drowned in a well, that turns up again as lively as ever. Any news of the baroness and the young ladies?"

"A letter," said he. "Come, get off your horse. I shall read to you the letter."

"Tell me — how were they taken?"

I was leading my horse, and we were walking through the deep grove.

"Eh bien, I am not able to tell," said he, shaking his head soberly. "You remember that morning — well, I have twenty men there for two days. They are armed, they surround the Hermitage, they keep a good watch. The wasp he is very troublesome, but they see no soldier. They stay, they burn the smudge. By and by I think there is nothing to fear, and I bring them home, but I leave three men. The baroness and the two girls and their servants they stay awhile to pack the trunk. They are coming to the château. It is in the evening; the coach is at the door; the servants have started. Suddenly — the British! I do not know how many. They come out of the woods like a lightning, and *bang! bang! bang!* they have killed my men. They take the baroness and the Misses de Lambert, and they drive away with them. The servants they hear the shots, they return, they come, and they tell us. We follow. We find the coach; it is in the road, by the north trail. Dieu! they are all gone! We travel to the river, but — " here he lifted his shoulders and shook his head dolefully — "we could do nothing."

"The general may let me go after them with a force of cavalry," I said. "I want you to come with me and talk to him."

"No, no, my capitaine!" said he; "it would

not be wise. We must wait. We do not know where they are. I have friends in Canada; they are doing their best, and when we hear from them — eh bien, we shall know what is necessary."

I told him how I had met them that night in Canada, and what came of it.

"They are a cruel people, the English," said he. "I am afraid to find them will be a matter of great difficulty."

"But the letter — "

"Ah, the letter," he interrupted, feeling in his pocket. "The letter is not much. It is from Tiptoes — from Louison. It was mailed this side of the river at Morristown. You shall see; they do not know where they are."

He handed me the letter. I read it with an eagerness I could not conceal. It went as follows: —

"MY DEAR COUNT: If this letter reaches you, it will, I hope, relieve your anxiety. We are alive and well, but where? I am sure I have no better idea than if I were a baby just born. We came here with our eyes covered after a long ride from the river, which we crossed in the night. I think it must have taken us three days to come here. We are shut up in a big house with high walls and trees and gardens around it — a beautiful place. We have fine beds and everything to eat, only we miss the bouillabaisse, and the jokes of M. Pidgeon, and the fine old claret. A fat Englishwoman who waddles around like a big goose and who calls me Mumm (as if I were a wine-maker!) waits upon us. We do not know the name of our host. He is a tall man who says little and has hair on his neck and on the back of his hands. Dieu! he is a lord who talks as if he were too lazy to breathe. It is 'Your Lordship this' and 'Your Lordship that.' But I must speak well of him, because he is going to read this letter: it is on that condition I am permitted to write. Therefore I say he is a great and good man, a beautiful man. The baroness and Louise send love to all. Madame says do not worry; we shall come out all right: but I say *worry!* and, good man, do not cease to worry until we are safe home. Tell the curé he has something to do now. I have worn out my rosary, and am losing faith. Tell him to try his.

"Your affectionate

"LOUISON."

"She is an odd girl," said the count, as I gave back the letter, "so full of fun, so happy, so bright, so quick — always on her tiptoes. Come, you are tired; you have ridden far in the dust. I shall make you glad to be here."

A groom took my horse, and the count led me down a wooded slope to the lakeside. Octagonal water-houses, painted white, lay floating at anchor near us. He rowed me to one of them for a bath. Inside was a rug and a table and soap and linen. A broad panel on a side of the floor came up as I pulled a cord, showing water clear and luminous to the sandy lake-bottom. The glow of the noonday filled the lake to its shores, and in a moment I clove the sunlit depths — a rare delight after my long, hot ride.

At luncheon we talked of the war, and he made much complaint of the Northern army, as did everybody those days.

"My boy," said he, "you should join Perry on the second lake. It is your only chance to fight; to win glory."

He told me then of the impending battle and of Perry's great need of men. I had read of the sea-fighting and longed for a part in it. To climb on hostile decks and fight hand to hand was a thing to my fancy. Ah, well! I was young then. At the count's table that day I determined to go, if I could get leave.

Thérèse and a young Parisienne, her friend, were at luncheon with us. They bade us adieu and went away for a gallop as we took cigars. We had no sooner left the dining room than I called for my horse. Due at the Harbor that evening, I could give myself no longer to the fine hospitality of the count. In a few moments I was bounding over the road, now cool in deep forest shadows. A little way on I overtook Thérèse and the Parisienne. The former called to me as I passed. I drew rein, coming back and stopping beside her. The other went on at a walk.

" M'sieur le Capitaine, have you any news of them — of Louise and Louison ? " she inquired. "You and my father were so busy talking I could not ask you before."

" I know this only: they are in captivity somewhere, I cannot tell where."

"You look worried, M'sieur le Capitaine; you have not the happy face, the merry look, any longer. In June you were a boy, in August

— voilà! it is a man! Perhaps you are preparing for the ministry."

She assumed a solemn look, glancing up at me as if in mockery of my sober face. She was a slim, fine brunette, who, as I knew, had long been a confidante of Louison.

"Alas! ma'm'selle, I am worried. I have no longer any peace."

"Do you miss them?" she inquired, a knowing look in her handsome eyes. "Do not think me impertinent."

"More than I miss my mother," I said.

"I have a letter," said she, smiling. "I do not know — I thought I should show it to you, but — but not to-day."

"Is it from them?"

"It is from Louison — from Tiptoes."

"And — and it speaks of me?"

"Ah, m'sieur," said she, arching her brows, "it has indeed much to say of you."

"And — and may I not see it?" I asked eagerly. "Ma'm'selle, I tell you I — I must see it."

"Why?" She stirred the mane of her horse with a red riding-whip.

"Why not?" I inquired, my heart beating fast.

"If I knew — if I were justified — you know I am her friend. I know all her secrets."

"Will you not be my friend also?" I interrupted.

"A friend of Louison, he is mine," said she.

"Ah, ma'm'selle, then I confess to you — it is because I love her."

"I knew it; I am no fool," was her answer. "But I had to hear it from you. It is a remarkable thing to do, but they are in such peril. I think you ought to know."

She took the letter from her bosom, passing it to my hand. A faint odor of violets came with it. It read: —

"MY DEAR THÉRÈSE: I wish I could see you, if only for an hour. I have so much to say. I have written your father of our prison home. I am going to write you of my troubles. You know what we were talking about the last time I saw you — myself and that handsome fellow. Mon Dieu! I shall not name him. It is not necessary. Well, you were right, my dear. I was a fool; I laughed at your warning; I did

not know the meaning of that delicious pain.
But oh, my dear friend, it has become a terrible
thing since I know I may never see him again.
My heart is breaking with it. Mère de Dieu!
I can no longer laugh or jest or pretend to be
happy. What shall I say? That I had rather
die than live without him? No; that is not
enough. I had rather be an old maid and live
only with the thought of *him* than marry another, if he were a king. I remember those
words of yours, 'I know he loves you.' Oh, my
dear Thérèse, what a comfort they are to me
now! I repeat them often. If *I* could only
say, 'I know'! Alas! I can but say, 'I do not
know,' nay, even, 'I do not believe.' If I had
not been a fool I should have made him tell me,
for I had him over his ears in love with me one
day, or I am no judge of a man. But, you know,
they are so fickle! And then the Yankee girls
are pretty and so clever. Well, they shall not
have him if I can help it. When I return there
shall be war, if necessary, between France and
America. And, Thérèse, you know I have
weapons, and you have done me the honor to
say I know how to use them. I have told
Louise, and — what do you think? — the poor
thing cried an hour — for pity of me! As ever,
she makes my trouble her own. I have been
selfish always, but I know the cure. It is love

— toujours l'amour.   Now I think only of him,
and he recalls you and your sweet words.   God
make you a true prophet!   With love to you
and the marquis, I kiss each line, praying for
happiness for you and for him.   Believe me as
ever,

" Your affectionate

" LOUISON.

"P.S.   I feel better now I have told you.   I
wonder what his Lordship will say.   Poor thing!
he will read this ; he will think me a fool.   Eh
bien, I have no better thought of him.   He can
put me under lock and key, but he shall not
imprison my secrets ; and, if they bore him, he
should not read my letters.   L."

I read it thrice, and held it for a moment to
my lips.   Every word stung me with the sweet
pain that afflicted its author.   I could feel my
cheeks burning.

"Ma'm'selle, pardon me ; it is not I she refers
to.   She does not say whom."

"Surely," said Thérèse, flirting her whip and
lifting her shoulders.   "M'sieur le Capitaine is
never a stupid man.   You — you should say
something very nice now."

"If it is I — thank God!   Her misery is my
delight, her liberation my one purpose."

"And my congratulations," said she, giving me her hand. "She has wit and beauty, a true heart, a great fortune, and — good luck in having your love."

I raised my hat, blushing to the roots of my hair.

"It is a pretty compliment," I said. "And — and I have no gift of speech to thank you. I am not a match for you except in my love of kindness and — and of Louison. You have made me happier than I have been before."

"If I have made you alert, ingenious, determined, I am content," was her answer. "I know you have courage."

"And will to use it."

"Good luck and adieu!" said she, with a fine flourish of her whip; those people had always a pretty politeness of manner.

"Adieu," I said, lifting my hat as I rode off, with a prick of the spur, for the road was long and I had lost quite half an hour.

My elation gave way to sober thought presently. I began to think of Louise — that quiet, frank, noble, beautiful, great-hearted girl, who might be suffering what trouble I knew not, and all silently, there in her prison home. A sadness grew in me, and then suddenly I saw the shadow of great trouble. I loved them both; I knew not which I loved the better. Yet this interview had almost committed me to Louison.

RDERS came shortly from the War Department providing a detail to go and help man the guns of Perry at Put-in Bay. I had the honor of leading them on the journey and turning them over to the young captain. I could not bear to be lying idle at the garrison. A thought of those in captivity was with me night and day, but I could do nothing for them. I had had a friendly talk with General Brown. He invited and received my confidence touching the tender solicitude I was unable to cover. I laid before him the plan of an expedition. He smiled, puffing a cigar thoughtfully.

"Reckless folly, Bell," said he, after a moment. "You are young and lucky. If you were flung in the broad water there with a millstone tied to your neck, I should not be surprised to see you turn up again. My young friend, to start off with no destination but Canada is too much even for you. We have no men to waste. Wait; a rusting sabre is better than a hole in the heart. There will be good work for you in a few days, I hope."

And there was — the job of which I have spoken, that came to me through his kind offices. We set sail in a schooner one bright morning, — D'ri and I and thirty others, — bound for Two-Mile Creek. Horses were waiting for us there. We mounted them, and made the long journey overland — a ride through wood and swale on a road worn by the wagons of the emigrant, who, even then, was pushing westward to the fertile valleys of Ohio. It was hard travelling, but that was the heyday of my youth, and the bird music, and the many voices of a waning summer in field and forest, were somehow in harmony with the great song of my heart. In the middle of the afternoon of September 6, we came to the Bay, and pulled up at headquarters, a two-story frame building on a high shore. There were wooded islands in the offing, and between them we could see the fleet — nine vessels, big and little.

I turned over the men, who were taken to the ships immediately and put under drill. Surgeon Usher of the *Lawrence* and a young midshipman rowed me to Gibraltar Island, well out in the harbor, where the surgeon presented me to Perry — a tall, shapely man, with dark hair and eyes, and ears hidden by heavy tufts of beard. He stood on a rocky point high above the water, a glass to his eye, looking seaward. His youth surprised me : he was then twenty-eight. I had read much of him and was looking for an older man. He received me kindly : he had a fine dignity and gentle manners. Somewhere he had read of that scrape of mine — the last one there among the Avengers. He gave my hand a squeeze and my sword a compliment I have not yet forgotten, assuring me of his pleasure that I was to be with him awhile. The greeting over, we rowed away to the *Lawrence*. She was chopping lazily at anchor in a light breeze, her sails loose. Her crew cheered their commander as we came under the frowning guns.

" They 're tired of waiting," said he ; " they 're looking for business when I come aboard."

He showed me over the clean decks : it was all as clean as a Puritan parlor.

"Captain," said he, " tie yourself to that big bow gun. It's the modern sling of David, only its pebble is big as a rock. Learn how to handle it, and you may take a fling at the British some day."

He put D'ri in my squad, as I requested, leaving me with the gunners. I went to work at once, and knew shortly how to handle the big machine. D'ri and I convinced the captain with no difficulty that we were fit for a fight so soon as it might come.

It came sooner than we expected. The cry of " Sail ho ! " woke me early one morning. It was the 10th of September. The enemy was coming. Sails were sticking out of the misty dawn a few miles away. In a moment our decks were black and noisy with the hundred and two that manned the vessel. It was every hand to rope and windlass then. Sails went up with a snap all around us, and the creak of blocks sounded far and near. In twelve minutes we were under way, leading the van to battle. The sun came up, lighting the great towers of canvas. Every vessel was now feeling for the wind, some with oars and sweeps to aid them. A light breeze came out of the southwest. Perry stood near me, his hat in his hand. He was looking back at the *Niagara*.

" Run to the leeward of the islands," said he to the sailing-master.

" Then you'll have to fight to the leeward," said the latter.

" Don't care, so long as we fight," said Perry. "Windward or leeward, we want to fight."

Then came the signal to change our course. The wind shifting to the southeast, we were all able to clear the islands and keep the weather-gage. A cloud came over the sun; far away the mist thickened. The enemy wallowed to the topsails, and went out of sight. We had lost the wind. Our sails went limp; flag and pennant hung lifeless. A light rain drizzled down, breaking the smooth plane of water into crowding rings and bubbles. Perry stood out in the drizzle as we lay waiting. All eyes were turning to the sky and to Perry. He had a look of worry and disgust. He was out for a quarrel, though the surgeon said he was in more need of physic, having the fever of malaria as well as that of war. He stood there, tall and hand-some, in a loose jacket of blue nankeen, with no sign of weakness in him, his eyes flashing as he looked up at the sky.

D'ri and I stood in the squad at the bow gun. D'ri was wearing an old straw hat; his flannel shirt was open at the collar.

"Ship stan's luk an ol' cow chawin' 'er cud," said he, looking off at the weather. "They's a win' comin' over there. It'll give 'er a slap 'n th' side purty soon, mebbe. Then she'll switch 'er tail 'n' go on 'bout 'er business."

In a moment we heard a roaring cheer back amidships. Perry had come up the companion-way with his blue battle-flag. He held it before him at arm's-length. I could see a part of its legend, in white letters, "Don't give up the ship."

"My brave lads," he shouted, "shall we hoist it?"

Our "Ay, ay, sir!" could have been heard a mile away, and the flag rose, above tossing hats and howling voices, to the mainroyalmast-head.

The wind came; we could hear the sails snap and stiffen as it overhauled the fleet behind us. In a jiffy it bunted our own hull and canvas, and again we began to plough the water. It grew into a smart breeze, and scattered the fleet of clouds that hovered over us. The rain passed; sunlight sparkled on the rippling plane of water. We could now see the enemy; he had hove to, and was waiting for us in a line. A crowd was gathering on the high shores we had left to see the battle. We were well in advance, crowding our canvas in a good breeze. I could hear only the roaring furrows of water on each side of the prow. Every man of us held his tongue, mentally trimming ship, as they say, for whatever might come. Three men scuffed by, sanding the decks. D'ri was leaning placidly over the big gun. He looked off at the white line, squinted knowingly, and spat over the bulwarks. Then he straightened up, tilting his hat to his right ear.

"They 're p'intin' their guns," said a swabber.

"Fust they know they 'll git spit on," said D'ri, calmly.

Well, for two hours it was all creeping and talking under the breath, and here and there an

oath as some nervous chap tightened the ropes
of his resolution. Then suddenly, as we swung
about, a murmur went up and down the deck.
We could see with our naked eyes the men who
were to give us battle. Perry shouted sternly
to some gunners who thought it high time to
fire. Then word came : there would be no firing until we got close. Little gusts of music
came chasing over the water faint-footed to our
decks — a band playing " Rule Britannia." I
was looking at a brig in the line of the enemy
when a bolt of fire leaped out of her and thick
belches of smoke rushed to her topsails. Then
something hit the sea near by a great hissing
slap, and we turned quickly to see chunks of
the shattered lake surface fly up in nets of spray
and fall roaring on our deck. We were all
drenched there at the bow gun. I remember
some of those water-drops had the sting of hard-
flung pebbles, but we only bent our heads,
waiting eagerly for the word to fire.

"We was th' ones 'at got spit on," said a
gunner, looking at D'ri.

"Wish they'd let us holler back," said the
latter, placidly. "Sick o' holdin' in."

We kept fanning down upon the enemy, now little more than a mile away, signalling the fleet to follow.

"My God! see there!" a gunner shouted.

The British line had turned into a reeling, whirling ridge of smoke lifting over spurts of flame at the bottom. We knew what was coming. Untried in the perils of shot and shell, some of my gunners stooped to cover under the bulwarks.

"Pull 'em out o' there," I called, turning to D'ri, who stood beside me.

The storm of iron hit us. A heavy ball crashed into the after bulwarks, tearing them away and slamming over gun and carriage, that slid a space, grinding the gunners under it. One end of a bowline whipped over us; a jib dropped; a brace fell crawling over my shoulders like a big snake; the foremast went into splinters a few feet above the deck, its top falling over, its canvas sagging in great folds. It was all the work of a second. That hasty flight of iron, coming out of the air, thick as a flock of pigeons, had gone through hull and rigging in a wink of the eye. And a fine mess it had made.

Men lay scattered along the deck, bleeding, yelling, struggling. There were two lying near us with blood spurting out of their necks. One rose upon a knee, choking horribly, shaken with the last throes of his flooded heart, and reeled over. The *Scorpion* of our fleet had got her guns in action; the little *Ariel* was also firing. D'ri leaned over, shouting in my ear.

"Don't like th' way they're whalin' uv us," he said, his cheeks red with anger.

"Nor I," was my answer.

"Don't like t' stan' here an' dew nuthin' but git licked," he went on. "'T ain' no way nat'ral."

Perry came hurrying forward.

"Fire!" he commanded, with a quick gesture, and we began to warm up our big twenty-pounder there in the bow. But the deadly scuds of iron kept flying over and upon our deck, bursting into awful showers of bolt and chain and spike and hammerheads. We saw shortly that our brig was badly out of gear. She began to drift to leeward, and being unable to aim at the enemy, we could make no use of the bow gun. Every brace and bowline cut

away, her canvas torn to rags, her hull shot
through, and half her men dead or wounded,
she was, indeed, a sorry sight. The *Niagara*
went by on the safe side of us, heedless of our
plight. Perry stood near, cursing as he looked
off at her. Two of my gunners had been hurt
by bursting canister. D'ri and I picked them
up, and made for the cockpit. D'ri's man kept
howling and kicking. As we hurried over the
bloody deck, there came a mighty crash beside
us and a burst of old iron that tumbled me to
my knees.

A cloud of smoke covered us. I felt the man
I bore struggle and then go limp in my arms; I
felt my knees getting warm and wet. The
smoke rose; the tall, herculean back of D'ri
was just ahead of me. His sleeve had been
ripped away from shoulder to elbow, and a spray
of blood from his upper arm was flying back
upon me. His hat crown had been torn off,
and there was a big rent in his trousers, but he
kept going. I saw my man had been killed in
my arms by a piece of chain, buried to its last
link in his breast. I was so confused by the
shock of it all that I had not the sense to lay

him down, but followed D'ri to the cockpit. He stumbled on the stairs, falling heavily with his burden. Then I dropped my poor gunner and helped them carry D'ri to a table, where they bade me lie down beside him.

"It is no time for jesting," said I, with some dignity.

"My dear fellow," the surgeon answered, "your wound is no jest. You are not fit for duty."

I looked down at the big hole in my trousers and the cut in my thigh, of which I had known nothing until then. I had no sooner seen it and the blood than I saw that I also was in some need of repair, and lay down with a quick sense of faintness. My wound was no pretty thing to see, but was of little consequence, a missile having torn the surface only. I was able to help Surgeon Usher as he caught the severed veins and bathed the bloody strands of muscle in D'ri's arm, while another dressed my thigh. That room was full of the wounded, some lying on the floor, some standing, some stretched upon cots and tables. Every moment they were crowding down the companionway with others. The cannonading was now so close and heavy that it gave me an ache in the ears, but above its quaking thunder I could hear the shrill cries of men sinking to hasty death in the grip of pain. The brig was in sore distress, her timbers creaking, snapping, quivering, like one being beaten to death, his bones cracking, his muscles pulping under heavy blows. We were above water-line there in the cockpit; we could feel her flinch and stagger. On her side there came suddenly a crushing blow, as if some great hammer, swung far in the sky, had come down upon her. I could hear the split and break of heavy timbers; I could see splinters flying over me in a rush of smoke, and the legs of a man go bumping on the beams above. Then came another crash of timbers on the port side. I leaped off the table and ran, limping, to the deck, I do not know why; I was driven by some quick and irresistible impulse. I was near out of my head, anyway, with the rage of battle in me and no chance to fight. Well, suddenly, I found myself stumbling, with drawn sabre, over heaps of the hurt and dead there on our reeking deck. It was a horrible place:

everything tipped over, man and gun and mast
and bulwark. The air was full of smoke, but
near me I could see a topsail of the enemy.
Balls were now plunging in the water alongside,
the spray drenching our deck. Some poor man
lying low among the dead caught me by the
boot-leg with an appealing gesture. I took hold
of his collar, dragging him to the cockpit. The
surgeon had just finished with D'ri. His arm
was now in sling and bandages. He was lying
on his back, the good arm over his face. There
was a lull in the cannonading. I went quickly
to his side.

"How are you feeling?" I asked, giving his
hand a good grip.

"Nuthin' t' brag uv," he answered. "Never
see nobody git hell rose with 'em s' quick es we
did — never."

Just then we heard the voice of Perry. He
stood on the stairs calling into the cockpit.

"Can any wounded man below there pull a
rope?" he shouted.

D'ri was on his feet in a jiffy, and we were
both clambering to the deck as another scud of
junk went over us. Perry was trying, with

block and tackle, to mount a carronade. A
handful of men were helping him. D'ri rushed
to the ropes, I following, and we both pulled
with a will. A sailor who had been hit in the
legs hobbled up, asking for room on the rope.
I told him he could be of no use, but he spat an
oath, and pointing at my leg, which was now
bleeding, swore he was sounder than I, and put
up his fists to prove it. I have seen no better
show of pluck in all my fighting, nor any that
ever gave me a greater pride of my own people
and my country. War is a great evil, I begin
to think, but there is nothing finer than the sight
of a man who, forgetting himself, rushes into
the shadow of death for the sake of something
that is better. At every heave on the rope
our blood came out of us, until a ball shattered a pulley, and the gun fell. Perry had
then a fierce look, but his words were cool, his
manner dauntless. He peered through lifting
clouds of smoke at our line. He stood near me,
and his head was bare. He crossed the littered
deck, his battle-flag and broad pennant that an
orderly had brought him trailing from his shoulder. He halted by a boat swung at the davits

" *D'ri, shaking a bloody, tattered flag, shouted:*
' *We'll tek care o' the ol' brig.*' "

on the port side — the only one that had not
gone to splinters.   There he called a crew about
him, and all got quickly aboard the boat — seven
besides the younger brother of Captain Perry
— and lowered it.   Word flew that he was leaving to take command of the sister brig, the
Niagara, which lay off a quarter of a mile or so
from where we stood.   We all wished to go,
but he would have only sound men; there were
not a dozen on the ship who had all their blood
in them.   As they pulled away, Perry standing
in the stern, D'ri lifted a bloody, tattered flag,
and leaning from the bulwarks, shook it over
them, cheering loudly.

"Give 'em hell!" he shouted.   "We'll tek
care o' the ol' brig."

We were all crying, we poor devils that were
left behind.   One, a mere boy, stood near me
swinging his hat above his head, cheering.   Hat
and hand fell to the deck as I turned to him.
He was reeling, when D'ri caught him quickly
with his good arm and bore him to the cockpit.

The little boat was barely a length off when
heavy shot fell splashing in her wake.   Soon
they were dropping all around her.   One crossed

her bow, ripping a long furrow in the sea. A
chip flew off her stern; a lift of splinters from
an oar scattered behind her. Plunging missiles
marked her course with a plait of foam, but she
rode on bravely. We saw her groping under
the smoke clouds; we saw her nearing the other
brig, and were all on tiptoe. The air cleared
a little, and we could see them ship oars and
go up the side. Then we set our blood dripping with cheers again, we who were wounded
there on the deck of the *Lawrence*. Lieutenant Yarnell ordered her one flag down. As it
sank fluttering, we groaned. Our dismay went
quickly from man to man. Presently we could
hear the cries of the wounded there below. A
man came staggering out of the cockpit, and
fell to his hands and knees, creeping toward us
and protesting fiercely, the blood dripping from
his mouth between curses.

"Another shot would sink her," Yarnell
shouted.

"Let 'er sink, d—n 'er," said D'ri. "Wish
t' God I c'u'd put my foot through 'er bottom.
When the flag goes down I wan' t' go tew."

The British turned their guns; we were no

longer in the smoky paths of thundering canister. The *Niagara* was now under fire. We
could see the dogs of war rushing at her in
leashes of flame and smoke. Our little gunboats, urged by oar and sweep, were hastening
to the battle front. We could see their men,
waist-high above bulwarks, firing as they came.
The *Detroit* and the *Queen Charlotte*, two heavy
brigs of the British line, had run afoul of each
other. The *Niagara*, signalling for close action,
bore down upon them. Crossing the bow of
one ship and the stern of the other, she raked
them with broadsides. We saw braces fly and
masts fall in the volley. The *Niagara* sheered
off, pouring shoals of metal on a British schooner,
stripping her bare. Our little boats had come
up, and were boring into the brigs. In a brief
time — it was then near three o'clock — a white
flag, at the end of a boarding-pike, fluttered
over a British deck. D'ri, who had been sitting
awhile, was now up and cheering as he waved
his crownless hat. He had lent his flag, and, in
the flurry, some one dropped it overboard. D'ri
saw it fall, and before we could stop him he had
leaped into the sea. I hastened to his help,

tossing a rope's end as he came up, swimming
with one arm, the flag in his teeth. I towed
him to the landing-stair and helped him over.
Leaning on my shoulder, he shook out the
tattered flag, its white laced with his own blood.

"Ready t' jump in hell fer thet ol' rag any
day," said he, as we all cheered him.

Each grabbed a tatter of the good flag, pressing hard upon D'ri, and put it to his lips and
kissed it proudly. Then we marched up and
down, D'ri waving it above us — a bloody squad
as ever walked, shouting loudly. D'ri had begun to weaken with loss of blood, so I coaxed
him to go below with me.

The battle was over; a Yankee band was
playing near by.

"Perry is coming! Perry is coming!" we
heard them shouting above.

A feeble cry that had in it pride and joy and
inextinguishable devotion passed many a fevered
lip in the cockpit.

There were those near who had won a better
peace, and they lay as a man that listens to
what were now the merest vanity.

Perry came, when the sun was low, with a

number of British officers, and received their surrender on his own bloody deck. I remember, as they stood by the ruined bulwarks and looked down upon tokens of wreck and slaughter, a dog began howling dismally in the cockpit.

I T was a lucky and a stubborn sea-fight. More blood to the number I never saw than fell on the *Lawrence*, eighty-three of our hundred and two men having been killed or laid up for repair. One has to search a bit for record of a more wicked fire. But we deserve not all the glory some histories have bestowed, for we had a larger fleet and better, if fewer, guns. It was, however, a thing to be proud of, that victory of the young captain. Our men, of whom many were raw recruits, — farmers and woodsmen, — stood to their work with splendid valor, and, for us in the North, it came near being decisive. D'ri and I were so put out of business that no part of the glory was ours, albeit we were praised in orders for valor under fire. But for both I say we had never less pride of ourselves in any

affair we had had to do with. Well, as I have said before, we were ever at our best with a sabre, and big guns were out of our line.

We went into hospital awhile, D'ri having caught cold and gone out of his head with fever. We had need of a spell on our backs, for what with all our steeplechasing over yawning graves — that is the way I always think of it — we were somewhat out of breath. No news had reached me of the count or the young ladies, and I took some worry to bed with me, but was up in a week and ready for more trouble. I had to sit with D'ri awhile before he could mount a horse.

September was nearing its last day when we got off a brig at the Harbor. We were no sooner at the dock than some one began to tell us of a new plan for the invasion of Canada. I knew Brown had had no part in it, for he said in my hearing once that it was too big a chunk to bite off.

There were letters from the count and Thé-rèse, his daughter. They had news for me, and would I not ride over as soon as I had returned? My mother — dearest and best of mothers — had

written me, and her tenderness cut me like a
sword for the way I had neglected her. Well,
it is ever so with a young man whose heart has
found a new queen. I took the missive with
wet eyes to our good farmer-general of the
North. He read it, and spoke with feeling of
his own mother gone to her long rest.

"Bell," said he, "you are worn out. After
mess in the morning mount your horses, you and
the corporal, and go and visit them. Report
here for duty on October 16."

Then, as ever after a kindness, he renewed
his quid of tobacco, turning quickly to the
littered desk at headquarters.

We mounted our own horses a fine, frosty
morning. The white earth glimmered in the
first touch of sunlight. All the fairy lanterns
of the frost king, hanging in the stubble and the
dead grass, glowed a brief time, flickered faintly,
and went out. Then the brown sward lay bare,
save in the shadows of rock or hill or forest that
were still white. A great glory had fallen over
the far-reaching woods. Looking down a long
valley, we could see towers of evergreen, ter-
races of red and brown, golden steeple-tops,

gilded domes minareted with lavender and purple and draped with scarlet banners. It seemed as if the trees were shriving after all the green riot of summer, and making ready for sackcloth and ashes. Some stood trembling, and as if drenched in their own blood. Now and then a head was bare and bent, and naked arms were lifted high, as if to implore mercy.

" Fine air," said I, breathing deep as we rode on slowly.

" 'T is sart'n," said D'ri. " Mother used t' say 'at the frost wus only the breath o' angels, an' when it melted it gin us a leetle o' the air o' heaven."

Of earth or heaven, it quickened us all with a new life. The horses fretted for their heads, and went off at a gallop, needing no cluck or spur. We pulled up at the château well before the luncheon hour. D'ri took the horses, and I was shown to the library, where the count came shortly, to give me hearty welcome.

" And what of the captives ? " I inquired, our greeting over.

" Alas! it is terrible; they have not returned,"

said he, "and I am in great trouble, for I have not written to France of their peril. Dieu! I hoped they would be soon released. They are well and now we have good news. Eh bien, we hope to see them soon. But of that Thérèse shall tell you. And you have had a terrible time on Lake Erie?"

He had read of the battle, but wanted my view of it. I told the story of the *Lawrence* and Perry; of what D'ri and I had hoped to do, and of what had been done to us. My account of D'ri — his droll comment, his valor, his misfortune — touched and tickled the count. He laughed, he clapped his hands, he shed tears of enthusiasm; then he rang a bell.

" The M'sieur D'ri — bring him here," said he to a servant.

D'ri came soon with a worried look, his trousers caught on his boot-tops, an old felt hat in his hand. Somehow he and his hat were as king and coronal in their mutual fitness; if he lost one, he swapped for another of about the same shade and shape. His brows were lifted, his eyes wide with watchful timidity. The count had opened a leather case and taken out of it a shiny disk of silver. He stepped to D'ri, and fastened it upon his waistcoat.

"'Pour la valeur éprouvée — de l'Empereur,'" said he, reading the inscription as he clapped him on the shoulder. "It was given to a soldier for bravery at Austerlitz by the great Napoleon," said he. "And, God rest him! the soldier he died of his wounds. And to me he have left the medal in trust for some man, the most brave, intrepid, honorable. M'sieur D'ri, I have the pleasure to put it where it belong."

D'ri shifted his weight, looking down at the medal and blushing like a boy.

"Much obleeged," he said presently. "Dunno but mebbe I better put it 'n my wallet. 'Fraid I 'll lose it off o' there."

He threw at me a glance of inquiry.

"No," said I, "do not bury your honors in a wallet."

He bowed stiffly, and, as he looked down at the medal, went away, spurs clattering.

Thérèse came in presently, her face full of vivacity and color.

"M'sieur le Capitaine," said she, "we are going for a little ride, the marquis and I. Will you come with us? You shall have the best horse in the stable."

"And you my best thanks for the honor," I said.

Our horses came up presently, and we all made off at a quick gallop. The forest avenues were now aglow and filled with hazy sunlight as with a flood, through which yellow leaves were slowly sinking. Our horses went to their fetlocks in a golden drift. The marquis rode on at a rapid pace, but soon Thérèse pulled rein, I keeping abreast of her.

In a moment our horses were walking quietly.

"You have news for me, ma'm'selle?" I remarked.

"Indeed, I have much news," said she, as always, in French. "I was afraid you were not coming in time, m'sieur."

She took a dainty letter from her bosom, passing it to me.

My old passion flashed up as I took the perfumed sheets. I felt my heart quicken, my face burn with it. I was to have good news at last of those I loved better than my life, those I had not forgotten a moment in all the peril of war.

I saw the handwriting of Louison and then a vision of her — the large eyes, the supple, splendid figure, the queenly bearing. It read : —

"MY DEAR THÉRÈSE: At last they promise to return us to you on the 12th of October. You are to send two men for us — not more — to the head of Eagle Island, off Ste. Roche, in the St. Lawrence, with canoes, at ten o'clock in the evening of that day. They will find a lantern hanging on a tree at the place we are to meet them. We may be delayed a little, but they are to wait for us there. And, as you love me, see that one is my brave captain — I do not care about the other who comes. First of all I wish to see my emperor, my love, the tall, handsome, and gallant youngster who has won me. What a finish for this odd romance if he only comes ! And then I do wish to see you, the count, and the others. I read your note with such a pleasure ! You are sure that he loves me ? And that he does not know that I love him ? I do not wish him to know, to suspect, until he has asked me to be his queen — until he has a right to know. Once he has my secret, Love is robbed of his best treasure. Mon Dieu ! I wish to tell him myself, sometime, if he ever has the cour-

age to take command of me. I warn you,
Thérèse, if I think he knows — when I see him
— I shall be cruel to him; I shall make him
hate me. So you see I will not be cheated of
my wooing, and I know you would not endanger
my life's happiness. I have written a little song
— for him. Well, some day I shall sing it to
him, and will he not be glad to know I could do
it? Here are the first lines to give you the
idea : —

> My emperor! my emperor!
>   Thy face is fair to see;
> Thy house is old, thy heart is gold,
>   Oh, take command of me!

> O emperor! my emperor!
>   Thy sceptre is of God;
> Through all my days I'll sing thy praise,
>   And tremble at thy nod.

But, dear Thérèse, you ought to hear the music;
I have quite surprised myself. Indeed, love is
a grand thing; it has made me nobler and
stronger. They really say I am not selfish any
more. But I am weary of waiting here, and so
eager to get home. You are in love, and you
have been through this counting of the hours.
We are very comfortable here, and they let us
go and come as we like inside the high walls.

I have told you there is a big, big grove and garden.

"We saw nothing of 'his Lordship' for weeks until three days ago, when they brought him here wounded. That is the reason we could not send you a letter before now. You know he has to see them all and arrange for their delivery. Well, he sent for Louise that day he came. She went to him badly frightened, poor thing! as, indeed, we all were. He lay in bed helpless, and wept when he saw her. She came back crying, and would not tell what he had said. I do think he loves her very dearly, and somehow we are all beginning to think better of him. Surely no one could be more courteous and gallant. Louise went to help nurse him yesterday, dear, sweet little mother! Then he told her the good news of our coming release, where your men would meet us, and all as I have written. He is up in his chair to-day, the maid tells me. I joked Louise about him this morning, and she began to cry at once, and said her heart was not hers to give. The sly thing! I wonder whom she loves; but she would say no more, and has had a long face all day. She is so stubborn! I have sworn I will never tell her another of my secrets. You are to answer quickly, sending your note by courier to the Indian dockman at Elizabethport, addressed

Robin Adair, Box 40, St. Hilière, Canada. And the love of all to all. Adieu.

> " Your loving
>
> " LOUISON.

" P.S. Can you tell me, is the captain of noble birth? I have never had any doubt of it, he is so splendid."

It filled me with a great happiness and a bitter pang. I was never in such a conflict of emotion.

"Well," said Thérèse, "do you see my trouble? Having shown you the first letter, I had also to show you the second. I fear I have done wrong. My soul —"

" Be blessed for the good tidings," I interrupted.

" Thanks. I was going to say it accuses me. Louison is a proud girl; she must never know. She can never know unless —"

"You tell her," said I, quickly. "And of course you will."

" What do you mean?" she asked.

" That every secret that must not be told is the same as published if — if —"

"If *what?*"

"If — if it tells a pretty story with some love in it," I said, with a quick sense of caution. "Ah, ma'm'selle, do I not know what has made your lips so red?"

"What may it be?"

"The attrition of many secrets — burning secrets," I said, laughing.

"Mordieu! what charming impudence!" said she, her large eyes glowing thoughtfully, with some look of surprise. "You do not know me, m'sieur. I have kept many secrets and know the trick."

"Ah, then I shall ask of you a great favor," said I — "that you keep my secret also, that you do not tell her of my love."

She wheeled her horse with a merry peal of laughter, hiding her face, now red as her glove.

"It is too late," said she. "I have written her."

We rode on, laughing. In spite of the serious character of her words, I fell a-quaking from crown to stirrup. I was now engaged to Louison, or as good as that, and, being a

man of honor, I must think no more of her
sister.

"I wrote her of your confession," said she,
"for I knew it would make her so happy; but,
you know, I did not tell of — of the circumstances."

"Well, it will make it all the easier for me,"
I said. "Ma'm'selle, I assure you — I am not
sorry."

"And, my friend, you are lucky: she is so
magnificent."

"Her face will be a study when I tell her."

"The splendor of it!" said she.

"And the surprise," I added, laughing.

"Ah, m'sieur, she will play her part well.
She is clever. That moment when the true
love comes and claims her it is the sweetest
in a woman's life."

A thought came flying through my brain
with the sting of an arrow.

"She must not be deceived. I have not any
noble blood in me. I am only the son of a sol-
dier-farmer, and have my fortune to make," said
I, quickly.

"That is only a little folly," she answered,

laughing. "Whether you be rich or poor, prince or peasant, she cares not a snap of her finger. Ciel! is she not a republican, has she not money enough?"

"Nevertheless, I beg you to say, in your letter, that I have nothing but my sword and my honor."

As we rode along I noted in my book the place and time we were to meet the captives. The marquis joined us at the Hermitage, where a stable-boy watered our horses. Three servants were still there, the others being now in the count's service.

If any place give me a day's happiness it is dear to me, and the where I find love is forever sacred. I like to stand where I stood thinking of it, and there I see that those dear moments are as much a part of me as of history. So while Thérèse and the marquis got off their horses for a little parley with the gardener, I cantered up the north trail to where I sat awhile that delightful summer day with Louise. The grotto had now a lattice roofing of bare branches. Leaves, as red as her blush, as golden as my memories, came rattling through it, falling with a faint rustle. The big woods were as a gloomy and deserted mansion, with the lonely cry of the wind above and a ghostly rustle within where had been love and song and laughter and all delight.

D'RI and I left the château that afternoon, putting up in the red tavern at Morristown about dusk.

My companion rode away proudly, the medal dangling at his waistcoat lapel.

"Jerushy Jane!" said he, presently, as he pulled rein. "Ain't a-goin' t' hev thet floppin' there so — meks me feel luk a bird. Don't seem nohow nat'ral. Wha' d' ye s'pose he gin me thet air thing fer?"

He was putting it away carefully in his wallet.

"As a token of respect for your bravery," said I.

His laughter roared in the still woods, making my horse lift and snort a little. It was never an easy job to break any horse to D'ri's laughter.

"It's *reedic'lous*," said he, thoughtfully, in a moment.

"Why?"

"'Cause fer the reason why they don't no man deserve nuthin' fer doin' what he'd orter," he answered, with a serious and determined look.

"You did well," said I, "and deserve anything you can get."

"Done my damdest!" said he. "But I didn't do nuthin' but git licked. Got shot an' tore an' slammed all over thet air deck, an' could n't do no harm t' nobody. Jes luk a hoss tied 'n the stall, an' a lot o' men whalin' 'im, an' a lot more tryin' t' scare 'im t' death."

"Wha' d' ye s'pose thet air thing 's made uv?" he inquired after a little silence.

"Silver," said I.

"Pure silver?"

"Undoubtedly," was my answer.

"Judas Priest!" said he, taking out his wallet again, to look at the trophy. "Thet air mus' be wuth suthin'."

"More than a year's salary," said I.

He looked up at me with a sharp whistle of surprise.

" Ain' no great hand fer sech flummydiddles," said he, as he put the medal away.

"It's a badge of honor," said I. "It shows you 're a brave man."

"Got 'nough on 'em," said D'ri. "This 'ere rip 'n the forehead 's 'bout all the badge I need."

"It's from the emperor — the great Napoleon," I said. "It's a mark of his pleasure."

"Wall, by Judas Priest!" said D'ri, "I would n't jump over a stump over a stun wall t' please no emp'ror, an' I would n't cut off my leetle finger fer a hull bushel basket o' them air. I hain't a-fightin' fer no honor."

"What then?" said I.

His face turned very sober. He pursed his lips, and spat across the ditch; then he gave his mouth a wipe, and glanced thoughtfully at the sky.

"Fer liberty," said he, with decision. "Same thing my father died fer."

Not to this day have I forgotten it, the answer of old D'ri, or the look of him as he spoke. I was only a reckless youth fighting for the love of peril and adventure, and with too little thought of the high purposes of my country.

The causes of the war were familiar to me; that proclamation of Mr. Madison had been discussed freely in our home, and I had felt some share in the indignation of D'ri and my father. This feeling had not been allayed by the bloody scenes in which I had had a part. Now I began to feel the great passion of the people, and was put to shame for a moment.

" Liberty — that is a grand thing to fight for," said I, after a brief pause.

" Swap my blood any time fer thet air," said D'ri. " I can fight sassy, but not fer no king but God A'mighty. Don't pay t' git all tore up less it 's fer suthin' purty middlin' vallyble. My life ain't wuth much, but, ye see, I hain't nuthin' else."

We rode awhile in sober thought, hearing only a sough of the wind above and the rustling hoof-beat of our horses in the rich harvest of the autumn woods. We were walking slowly over a stretch of bare moss when, at a sharp turn, we came suddenly in sight of a huge bear that sat facing us. I drew my pistol as we pulled rein, firing quickly. The bear ran away into the brush as I fired another shot.

"He's hit," said D'ri, leaping off and bidding me hold the bit. Then, with a long stride, he ran after the fleeing bear. I had been waiting near half an hour when D'ri came back slowly, with a downhearted look.

"'T ain' no use," said he. "Can't never git thet bear. He's got a flesh-wound high up in his hin' quarters, an' he's travellin' fast."

He took a fresh chew of tobacco and mounted his horse.

"Terrible pity!" he exclaimed, shaking his head with some trace of lingering sorrow. "Ray," said he, soberly, after a little silence, "when ye see a bear lookin' your way, ef ye want 'im, alwus shute at the end thet's *toward* ye."

There was no better bear-hunter in the north woods than D'ri, and to lose a bear was, for him, no light affliction.

"Can't never break a bear's neck by shutin' 'im in the hin' quarters," he remarked.

I made no answer.

"Might jest es well spit 'n 'is face," he added presently; "jest eggzac'ly."

This apt and forceful advice calmed a lingering sense of duty, and he rode on awhile in silence. The woods were glooming in the early dusk when he spoke again. Something revived his contempt of my education. He had been trailing after me, and suddenly I felt his knee.

"Tell ye this, Ray," said he, in a kindly tone. "Ef ye wan' t' git a bear, got t' mux 'im up a leetle for'ard — right up 'n the neighborhood uv 'is fo'c's'le. Don't dew no good t' shute 'is hams. Might es well try t' choke 'im t' death by pinchin' 'is tail."

We were out in the open. Roofs and smoking chimneys were silhouetted on the sky, and, halfway up a hill, we could see the candle-lights of the red tavern. There, in the bar, before blazing logs in a great fireplace, for the evening had come chilly, a table was laid for us, and we sat down with hearty happiness to tankards of old ale and a smoking haunch. I have never drunk or eaten with a better relish. There were half a dozen or so sitting about the bar, and all ears were for news of the army and all hands for our help. If we asked for more potatoes or ale, half of them rose to proclaim it. Between pipes of Virginia tobacco, and old sledge, and songs of love and daring, we had a memorable night. When we went to our room, near twelve o'clock, I told D'ri of our dear friends, who, all day, had been much in my thought.

"Wus the letter writ by her?" he inquired.

"Not a doubt of it."

"Then it's all right," said he. "A likely pair o' gals them air — no mistake."

"But I think they made me miss the bear," I answered.

"Ray," said D'ri, soberly, "when yer shutin' a bear, ef ye want 'im, don't never think o' nuthin' but the bear." Then, after a moment's pause, he added: "Won't never hev no luck killin' a bear ef ye don' quit dwellin' so on them air gals."

I thanked him, with a smile, and asked if he knew Eagle Island.

"Be'n all over it half a dozen times," said he. "'T ain' no more 'n twenty rod from the Yankee shore, thet air island ain't. We c'u'd paddle there in a day from our cove."

And that was the way we planned to go, —

by canoe from our landing, — and wait for the
hour at Paleyville, a Yankee village opposite
the island. We would hire a team there, and
convey the party by wagon to Leraysville.

We were off at daybreak, and going over the
hills at a lively gallop. Crossing to Caraway
Pike, in the Cedar Meadows, an hour later, we
stampeded a lot of moose. One of them, a
great bull, ran ahead of us, roaring with fright,
his antlers rattling upon bush and bough, his
black bell hanging to the fern-tops.

" Don' never wan' t' hev no argyment with one
o' them air chaps 'less ye know purty nigh how
't 's comin' out," said D'ri. " Alwus want a gun
es well es a purty middlin' ca-a-areful aim on
your side. Then ye 're apt t' need a tree, tew,
'fore ye git through with it." After a moment's
pause he added : " Got t' be a joemightyful stout
tree, er he 'll shake ye out uv it luk a ripe apple."

" They always have the negative side of the
question," I said. " Don't believe they 'd ever
chase a man if he 'd let 'em alone."

" Yis, siree, they would," was D'ri's answer.
" I 've hed 'em come right efter me 'fore ever I
c'u'd lift a gun. Ye see, they 're jest es cur'us

'bout a man es a man is 'bout them. Ef they
can't smell 'im, they're terrible cur'us. Jes'
wan' t' see what's inside uv 'im an' what kind
uv a smellin' critter he is. Dunno es they wan' t'
dew 'im any pertic'lar harm. Jes' wan' t' mux
'im over a leetle; but they dew it *awful careless*,
an' he ain't never fit t' be seen no more."

He snickered faintly as he spoke.

" An' they don't nobody see much uv 'im efter
thet, nuther," he added, with a smile.

" I 'member once a big bull tried t' find out the
kind o' works I hed in me. 'T wa'n' no moose —
jest a common ord'nary three-year-ol' bull."

"Hurt you?" I queried.

"No; 't hurt 'im," said he, soberly. "Sp'ilt
'im, es ye might say. Could n't never bear the
sight uv a man efter thet. Seem so he did n't
think he wus fit t' be seen. Nobody c'u'd ever
git 'n a mild o' th' poor cuss. Hed t' be shot."

"What happened?"

"Hed a stout club 'n my hand," said he.
" Got holt uv 'is tail, an' begun a-whalin' uv 'im.
Run 'im down a steep hill, an' passin' a tree, I
tuk one side an' he t' other. We parted there
fer the las' time."

He looked off at the sky a moment.

Then came his inevitable addendum, which was: "I hed a dam sight more tail 'an he did, thet 's sartin."

About ten o'clock we came in sight of our old home. Then we hurried our horses, and came up to the door with a rush. A stranger met us there.

"Are you Captain Bell?" said he, as I got off my horse.

I nodded.

"I am one of your father's tenants," he went on. "Ride over the ridge yonder about half a mile, and you will see his house." I looked at D'ri and he at me. He had grown pale suddenly, and I felt my own surprise turning into alarm.

"Are they well?" I queried.

"Very well, and looking for you," said he, smiling.

We were up in our saddles, dashing out of the yard in a jiffy. Beyond the ridge a wide mile of smooth country sloped to the river margin. Just off the road a great house lay long and low in fair acres. Its gables were red-roofed, its walls of graystone half hidden by lofty hedges of cedar. We stopped our horses, looking off to the distant woods on each side of us.

"Can't be," said D'ri, soberly, his eyes squinting in the sunlight.

"Wonder where they live," I remarked.

"All looks mighty cur'us," said he. "'T ain' no way nat'ral."

"Let's go in there and ask," I suggested.

We turned in at the big gate and rode silently over a driveway of smooth gravel to the door. In a moment I heard my father's hearty hello, and then my mother came out in a better gown than ever I had seen her wear. I was out of the saddle and she in my arms before a word was spoken. My father, hardy old Yankee, scolded the stamping horse, while I knew well he was only upbraiding his own weakness.

"Come, Ray; come, Darius," said my mother, as she wiped her eyes; "I will show you the new house."

A man took the horses, and we all followed her into the splendid hall, while I was filled with wonder and a mighty longing for the old home.

I T was a fine house — that in which I spent many happy years back in my young manhood. Not, indeed, so elegant and so large as this where I am now writing, but comfortable. To me, then, it had an atmosphere of romance and some look of grandeur. Well, in those days I had neither a sated eye, nor gout, nor judgment of good wine. It was I who gave it the name of Fairacres that day when, coming out of the war, we felt its peace and comfort for the first time, and, dumfounded with surprise, heard my mother tell the story of it.

"My grandfather," said she, "was the Chevalier Ramon Ducet de Trouville, a brave and gallant man who, for no good reason, disinherited my father. The property went to my uncle, the only other child of the chevalier, and he, as I have told you, wrote many kind letters to me, and sent each year a small gift of money. Well, he died before the war, — it was in March, — and, having no children, left half his fortune to me. You, Ramon, will remember that long before you went away to the war a stranger came to see me one day — a stout man, with white hair and dark eyes. Do you not remember? Well, I did not tell you then, because I was unable to believe, that he came to bring the good news. But he came again after you left us, and brought me money —- a draft on account. For us it was a very large sum, indeed. You know we have always been so poor, and we knew that when the war was over there would be more and a-plenty coming. So, what were we to do? 'We will build a home,' said I; 'we will enjoy life as much as possible. We will surprise Ramon. When he returns from the war he shall see it, and be very happy.' The architect came with the builders, and, voilà! the house is ready, and you are here, and after so long it is better than a fortune to see you. I thought you would never come."

She covered her face a moment, while my

father rose abruptly and left the room. I kissed the dear hands that long since had given to heavy toil their beauty and shapeliness.

But enough of this, for, after all, it is neither here nor there. Quick and unexpected fortune came to many a pioneer, as it came to my mother, by inheritance, as one may see if he look only at the records of one court of claims — that of the British.

"Before long you may wish to marry," said my mother, as she looked up at me proudly, "and you will not be ashamed to bring your wife here."

I vowed, then and there, I should make my own fortune, — I had Yankee enough in me for that, — but, as will be seen, the wealth of heart and purse my mother had, helped in the shaping of my destiny. In spite of my feeling, I know it began quickly to hasten the life-currents that bore me on. And I say, in tender remembrance of those very dear to me, I had never a more delightful time than when I sat by the new fireside with all my clan, — its number as yet undiminished, — or went roistering in wood or field with the younger children.

The day came when D'ri and I were to meet the ladies. We started early that morning of the 12th. Long before daylight we were moving rapidly down-river in our canoes.

I remember seeing a light flash up and die away in the moonlit mist of the river soon after starting.

"The boogy light!" D'ri whispered. "There 't goes ag'in!"

I had heard the river folk tell often of this weird thing — one of the odd phenomena of the St. Lawrence.

"Comes alwus where folks hev been drownded," said D'ri. "Thet air 's what I 've hearn tell."

It was, indeed, the accepted theory of the fishermen, albeit many saw in the boogy light a warning to mark the place of forgotten murder, and bore away.

The sun came up in a clear sky, and soon, far and wide, its light was tossing in the ripple-tops. We could see them glowing miles away. We were both armed with sabre and pistols, for that river was the very highway of adventure in those days of the war.

"Don' jes' like this kind uv a hoss," said D'ri. "Got t' keep whalin' 'im all the while, an' he's apt t' slobber 'n rough goin'."

He looked thoughtfully at the sun a breath, and then trimmed his remark with these words: "Ain't eggzac'ly sure-footed, nuther."

"Don't require much feed, though," I suggested.

"No; ye hev t' dew all the eatin', but ye can alwus eat 'nough fer both."

It was a fine day, and a ride to remember. We had a warm sun, a clear sky, and now and then we could feel the soft feet of the south wind romping over us in the river way. Here and there a swallow came coasting to the ripples, sprinkling the holy water of delight upon us, or a crow's shadow ploughed silently across our bows. It thrilled me to go cantering beside the noisy Rapides du Plats or the wild-footed Galloup, two troops of water hurrying to the mighty battles of the sea. We mounted reeling knolls, and coasted over whirling dips, and rushed to boiling levels, and jumped foamy ridges, and went galloping in the rush and tumble of long slopes.

"Let 'er rip!" I could hear D'ri shouting, once in a while, as he flashed up ahead of me. "Let 'er rip! Consarn 'er pictur'!"

He gave a great yell of triumph as we slowed in a long stretch of still, broad water. "Judas Priest!" said he, as I came alongside, "thet air 's rougher 'n the bog trail."

We came to Paleyville with time only for a bite of luncheon before dark. We could see no sign of life on the island or the "Canuck shore" as we turned our bows to the south channel. That evening the innkeeper sat with us under a creeking sign, our chairs tilted to the tavern-side.

D'ri was making a moose-horn of birch-bark as he smoked thoughtfully. When he had finished, he raised it to his lips and moved the flaring end in a wide circle as he blew a blast that rang miles away in the far forest.

"Ef we heppen t' git separated in any way, shape, er manner 'cept one," said he, as he slung it over his shoulder with a string, "ye 'll know purty nigh where I be when ye hear thet air thing."

"You said, 'in any way, shape, er manner

'cept one,'" I quoted. "What do you mean by that?"

My friend expectorated, looking off into the night soberly a moment.

"Guess I did n't mean nuthin'," said he, presently. "When I set out t' say suthin', don't never know where I'm goin' t' land. Good deal luk settin' sail without a compass. Thet 's one reason I don't never say much 'fore women."

Our good host hurried the lagging hours with many a tale of the river and that island we were soon to visit, once the refuge of Tadusac, the old river pirate, so he told us, with a cave now haunted by some ghost. We started for the shore near ten o'clock, the innkeeper leading us with a lantern, its light flickering in a west wind. The sky was cloudy, the night dark. Our host lent us the lantern, kindly offering to build a bonfire on the beach at eleven, to light us home.

"Careful, boys," said the innkeeper, as we got aboard. "Aim straight fer th' head o' th' island. Can't ye see it — right over yer heads there? 'Member, they 's awful rough water below."

We pushed off, D'ri leading. I could see

nothing of the island, but D'ri had better eyes, and kept calling me as he went ahead. After a few strokes of the paddle I could see on the dark sky the darker mass of tree-tops.

"Better light up," I suggested. We were now close in.

"Hush!" he hissed. Then, as I came up to him, he went on, whispering: "'T ain't bes' t' mek no noise here. Don' know none tew much 'bout this here business. Don' cal'late we 're goin' t' hev any trouble, but if we dew — Hark!"

We had both heard a stir in the bushes, and stuck our paddles in the sand, listening. After a little silence I heard D'ri get up and step stealthily into the water and buckle on his sword. Then I could hear him sinking the canoe and shoving her anchor deep into the sand. He did it with no noise that, fifty feet away, could have been distinguished from that of the ever-murmuring waters. In a moment he came and held my canoe, while I also took up my trusty blade, stepping out of the canoe into the shallow water. Then he shoved her off a little, and sank her beside the other. I knew not his purpose, and made no question of it, following him as he strode the shore with measured paces, the lantern upon his arm. Then presently he stuck his paddle into the bushes, and mine beside it. We were near the head of the island, walking on a reedy strip of soft earth at the river margin. After a few paces we halted to listen, but heard only the voice of the water and the murmur of pines. Then we pushed through a thicket of small fir trees to where we groped along in utter darkness among the big tree trunks on a muffle-footing. After a moment or so we got a spray of light. We halted, peering at the glow that now sprinkled out through many a pinhole aperture in a fairy lattice of pine needles.

My heart was beating loudly, for there was the promised lantern. Was I not soon to see the brighter light of those dear faces? It was all the kind of thing I enjoyed then, — the atmosphere of peril and romance, — wild youth that I was. It is a pity, God knows, I had so little consideration for old D'ri; but he loved me, and — well, he himself had some pleasure in excitement.

We halted for only a moment, pushing boldly through a thicket of young pines into the light. A lantern hung on the bough of a tall tree, and beneath it was a wide opening well carpeted with moss and needles. We peered off into the gloom, but saw nothing.

D'ri blew out a thoughtful breath, looking up into the air coolly, as he filled his pipe.

"Consarned if ever I wanted t' have a smoke s' bad 'n all my born days," he remarked.

Then he moved his holster, turned his scabbard, and sat down quietly, puffing his pipe with some look of weariness and reflection. We were sitting there less than five minutes when we heard a footfall near by ; then suddenly two men strode up to us in the dim light. I recognized at once the easy step, the long, lithe figure, of his Lordship in the dress of a citizen, saving sword and pistols.

"Ah, good evening, gentlemen," said he, quietly. "How are you?"

"Better than — than when we saw you last," I answered.

D'ri had not moved ; he looked up at me with a sympathetic smile.

"I presume," said his Lordship, in that familiar, lazy tone, as he lighted a cigar, "there was — ah — good room for improvement, was there not?"

"Abundant," said I, thoughtfully. "You were not in the best of health yourself that evening."

"True," said he; "I — I was in bad fettle and worse luck."

"How are the ladies?"

"Quite well," said he, blowing a long puff.

"Ready to deliver them?" I inquired.

"Presently," said he. "There are — some formalities."

"Which are — ?" I added quickly.

"A trifle of expenses and a condition," said he, lazily.

"How much, and what?" I inquired, as D'ri turned his ear.

"One thousand pounds," said his Lordship, quickly. "Not a penny more than this matter has cost me and his Majesty."

"What else?" said I.

"This man," he answered calmly, with a little gesture aimed at D'ri.

My friend rose, struck his palm with the
pipe-bowl, and put up his knife.

"Ef ye're goin' t' tek me," said he, "better
begin right off, er ye won't hev time 'fore
breakfust."

Then he clapped the moose-horn to his lips
and blew a mighty blast. It made the two men
jump and set the near thicket reeling. The
weird barytone went off moaning in the far
wastes of timber. Its rush of echoes had
begun. I put my hand to my sabre, for there
in the edge of the gloom I saw a thing that
stirred me to the marrow. The low firs were
moving toward us, root and branch, their twigs
falling. Gods of war! it made my hair stand
for a jiffy to see the very brush take feet and
legs. On sea or land I never saw a thing that
gave me so odd a feeling. We stood for a
breath or two, then started back, our sabres
flashing; for, as the twigs fell, we saw they
had been decorating a squad of the British.
They came on. I struck at the lantern, but too
late, for his Lordship had swung it away. He
stumbled, going to his knees; the lantern hit
the earth and went out. I had seen the squad

break, running each way, to surround us. D'ri grabbed my hand as the dark fell, and we went plunging through the little pines, hitting a man heavily, who fell grunting. We had begun to hear the rattle of boats, a shouting, and quick steps on the shore. We crouched a moment. D'ri blew the moose-horn, pulling me aside with him quickly after the blast. Lights were now flashing near. I could see little hope for us, and D'ri, I thought, had gone crazy. He ran at the oncomers, yelling, "Hey, Rube!" at the top of his lungs. I lay low in the brush a moment. They rushed by me, D'ri in the fore with fending sabre. A tawny hound was running in the lead, his nose down, baying loudly. Then I saw the truth, and made after them with all the speed of my legs. They hustled over the ridge, their lights flashing under. For a jiffy I could see only, here and there, a leaping glow in the tree-tops. I rushed on, passing one who had tumbled headlong. The lights below me scattered quickly and stopped. I heard a great yelling, a roar of muskets, and a clash of swords. A hush fell on them as I came near. Then I heard a voice that thrilled me.

"Your sword, sir!" it commanded.

"Stop," said I, sharply, coming near.

There stood my father in the lantern-light, his sword drawn, his gray hair stirring in the breeze. Before him was my old adversary, his Lordship, sword in hand. Near by, the squad of British, now surrounded, were giving up their arms. They had backed to the river's edge; I could hear it lapping their heels. His Lordship sneered, looking at the veteran who stood in a gray frock of homespun, for all the world, I fancy, like one of those old yeomen who fought with Cromwell.

"Your sword, sir," my father repeated.

"Pardon me," said the young man, with a fascinating coolness of manner, "but I shall have to trouble you —"

He hesitated, feeling his blade.

"How?" said my father.

"To fight for it," said his Lordship, quietly.

"Surrender — fool!" my father answered. "You cannot escape."

"Tut, tut!" said his Lordship. "I never heard so poor a compliment. Come in reach, and I shall make you think better of me."

"Give up your sword."

"After my life, then my sword," said he, with a quick thrust.

Before I could take a step, their swords were clashing in deadly combat. I rushed up to break in upon them, but the air was full of steel, and then my father needed no help. He was driving his man with fiery vigor. I had never seen him fight; all I had seen of his power had been mere play.

It was grand to see the old man fighting as if, for a moment, his youth had come back to him. I knew it could not go far. His fire would burn out quickly; then the blade of the young Britisher, tireless and quick as I knew it to be, would let his blood before my very eyes. What to do I knew not. Again I came up to them; but my father warned me off hotly. He was fighting with terrific energy. I swear to you that in half a minute he had broken the sword of his Lordship, who took to the water, swimming for his life. I leaped in, catching him half over the eddy, where we fought like madmen, striking in the air and bumping on the bottom. We were both near drowned when

D'ri swam out and gave me his belt-end, hauling us in.

I got to my feet soon. My father came
up to me, and wiped a cut on my forehead.

"Damn you, my boy!" said he. "Don't
ever interfere with me in a matter of that kind.
You might have been hurt."

We searched the island, high and low, for
the ladies, but with no success. Then we
marched our prisoners to the south channel,
where a bateau — the same that brought us
help — had been waiting. One of our men
had been shot in the shoulder, another gored
in the hip with a bayonet, and we left a young
Briton dead on the shore. We took our prisoners to Paleyville, and locked them overnight in
the blockhouse.

The channel was lighted by a big bonfire on
the south bank, as we came over. Its flames
went high, and made a great, sloping volcano of
light in the darkness.

After the posting of the guard, some gathered
about my father and began to cheer him. It
nettled the veteran. He would take no honor

for his defeat of the clever man, claiming the latter had no chance to fight.

"He had no foot-room with the boy one side and D'ri t' other," said he. "I had only to drive him back."

My father and the innkeeper and D'ri and I sat awhile, smoking, in the warm glow of the bonfire.

"You're a long-headed man," said I, turning to my comrade.

"Kind o' thought they'd be trouble," said D'ri. "So I tuk 'n ast yer father t' come over hossback with hef a dozen good men. They got three more et the tavern here, an' lay off 'n thet air bateau, waitin' fer the moose-call. I cal'lated I didn't want no more slidin' over there 'n Canady."

After a little snicker, he added: "Hed all 't wus good fer me the las' time. 'S a leetle tew swift."

"Gets rather scary when you see the bushes walk," I suggested.

"Seen whut wus up 'fore ever they med a move," said D'ri. "Them air bushes didn't look jest es nat'ral es they'd orter. Bet ye

they 're some o' them bushwhackers o' Fitzgibbon. Got loops all over their uniforms,
so ye c'u'd stick 'em full o' boughs. Jerushy!
never see nuthin' s' joemightful cur'us 'n all
my born days — never." He stopped a breath,
and then added: " Could n't be nuthin' cur'user
'n thet."

W E hired team and wagon of the innkeeper, and a man to paddle up-river and return with the horses.

I had a brief talk with our tall prisoner while they were making ready.

"A word of business, your Lordship," I said as he came out, yawning, with the guard.

"Ah, well," said he, with a shiver, "I hope it is not so cold as the air."

"It is hopeful; it is cheering," was my answer.

"And the topic?"

"An exchange — for the ladies."

He thought a moment, slapping the dust off him with a glove.

"This kind of thing is hard on the trousers," he remarked carelessly. "I will consider;

I think it could be arranged. Meanwhile, I give you my word of honor, you need have no worry."

We were off at daybreak with our prisoners; there were six of them in all. We put a fold of linen over the eyes of each, and roped them all together, so that they could sit or stand, as might please them, in the wagon-box.

"It's barbarity," said his Lordship, as we put on the fold. "You Yankees never knew how to treat a prisoner."

"Till you learnt us," said D'ri, quickly. "Couldn't never fergit thet lesson. Ef I hed my way 'bout you, I'd haul ye up t' th' top o' thet air dead pine over yender, 'n' let ye slide down."

"Rather too steep, I should say," said his Lordship, wearily.

"Ye wouldn't need no grease," said D'ri, with a chuckle.

We were four days going to the Harbor. My father and his men came with us, and he told us many a tale, that journey, of his adventures in the old war. We kept our promise, turning over the prisoners a little before sundown of the 16th. Each was given a great room and every possible comfort. I arranged soon for the release of all on the safe return of the ladies.

In the evening of the 17th his Lordship sent for me. He was a bit nervous, and desired a conference with the general and me. De Chaumont had been over to the headquarters that day in urgent counsel. He was weary of delay and planning an appeal to the French government. General Brown was prepared to give the matter all furtherance in his power, and sent quickly for the Englishman. They brought him over at nine o'clock. We uncovered his eyes and locked the door, and "gave him a crack at the old Madeira," as they used to say, and made him as comfortable as might be at the cheery fireside of the general.

"I've been thinking," said his Lordship, after a drink and a word of courtesy. I never saw a man of better breeding or more courage, I am free to say. "You may not agree it is possible, but, anyhow, I have been

trying to think. You have been decent to
me. I don't believe you are such a bad lot,
after all; and while I should be sorry to have
you think me tired of your hospitality, I desire
to hasten our plans a little. I propose an
exchange of — of — "

He hesitated, whipping the ashes off his
cigar.

"Well — first of confidence," he went on.
" I will take your word if you will take mine."

"In what matter?" the general inquired.

"That of the ladies and their relief," said
he. "A little confidence will — will — "

"Grease the wheels of progress?" the
general suggested, smiling.

"Quite so," he answered lazily. "To begin
with, they are not thirty miles away, if I am
correct in my judgment of this locality."

There was a moment of silence.

"My *dear* sir," he went on presently, "this
ground is quite familiar to me. I slept in
this very chamber long ago. But that is not
here nor there. Day after to-morrow, a little
before midnight, the ladies will be riding
on the shore pike. You could meet them

and bring them out to a schooner, I suppose
— if —"

He stopped again, puffing thoughtfully.

"If we could agree," he went on. "Now
this would be my view of it : You let me send
a messenger for the ladies. You would have
to take them by force somehow; but, you
know, I could make it easy — arrange the
time and place, no house near, no soldiers,
no resistance but that of the driver, who
should not share our confidence — no danger.
You take them to the boats and bring them
over ; but, first — "

He paused again, looking at the smoke-
rings above his head in a dreamy manner.

"'First,'" my chief repeated.

"Well," said he, leaning toward him with
a little gesture, "to me the word of a gentleman is sacred. I know you are both gentlemen. I ask for your word of honor."

"To what effect ?" the general queried.

"That you will put us safely on British
soil within a day after the ladies have arrived,"
said he.

"It is irregular and a matter of some

difficulty," said the general. "Whom would you send with such a message?"

"Well, I should say some Frenchwoman could do it. There must be one here who is clever enough."

"I know the very one," said I, with enthusiasm. "She is as smart and cunning as they make them."

"Very well," said the general; "that is but one step. Who is to capture them and take the risk of their own heads?"

"D'ri and I could do it alone," was my confident answer.

"Ah, well," said his Lordship, as he rose languidly and stood with his back to the fire, "I shall send them where the coast is clear — my word for that. Hang me if I fail to protect them."

"I do not wish to question your honor," said the general, "or violate in any way this atmosphere of fine courtesy; but, sir, I do not know you."

"Permit me to introduce myself," said the Englishman, as he ripped his coat-lining and drew out a folded sheet of purple parchment.

"I am Lord Ronley, fifth Earl of Pickford, and cousin of his Most Excellent Majesty the King of England; there is the proof."

He tossed the parchment to the table carelessly, resuming his chair.

"Forgive me," said he, as the general took it. "I have little taste for such theatricals. Necessity is my only excuse."

"It is enough," said the other. "I am glad to know you. I hope sometime we shall stop fighting each other — we of the same race and blood. It is unnatural."

"Give me your hand," said the Englishman, with heartier feeling than I had seen him show, as he advanced. "Amen! I say to you."

"Will you write your message? Here are ink and paper," said the general.

His Lordship sat down at the table and hurriedly wrote these letters: —

"PRESCOTT, ONTARIO, November 17, 1813.

"To SIR CHARLES GRAVLEIGH, The Weirs, above Landsmere, Wrentham, Frontenac County, Canada.

"MY DEAR GRAVLEIGH: Will you see that the baroness and her two wards, the Misses de

Lambert, are conveyed by my coach, on the evening of the 18th inst., to that certain point on the shore pike between Amsbury and Lakeside known as Burnt Ridge, there to wait back in the timber for my messenger? Tell them they are to be returned to their home, and give them my very best wishes. Lamson will drive, and let the bearer ride with the others.

> "Very truly yours,
> "RONLEY."

To whom it may concern.

"Mme. St. Jovite, the bearer, is on her way to my house at Wrentham, Frontenac County, second concession, with a despatch of urgent character. I shall be greatly favored by all who give her furtherance in this journey.

> "Respectfully, etc.,
> "Ronley,
> "Colonel of King's Guard."

For fear of a cipher, the general gave tantamount terms for each letter, and his Lordship rewrote them.

"I thought the name St. Jovite would be as good as any," he remarked.

The rendezvous was carefully mapped. The guard came, and his Lordship rose languidly.

" One thing more," said he. " Let the men go over without arms — if — if you will be so good."

" I shall consider that," said the general.

" And when shall the messenger start? "

" Within the hour, if possible," my chief answered.

As they went away, the general sat down with me for a moment, to discuss the matter.

EREIN is the story of the adventures of his Lordship's courier, known as Mme. St. Jovite, on and after the night of November 17, 1813, in Upper Canada. This account may be accepted as quite trustworthy, its writer having been known to me these many years, in the which neither I nor any of my friends have had occasion to doubt her veracity. The writer gave more details than are desirable, but the document is nothing more than a letter to an intimate friend. I remember well she had an eye for color and a taste for description not easy to repress.

When I decided to go it was near midnight. The mission was not all to my taste, but the reward was handsome and the letter of Lord Ronley reassuring. I knew I could do it, and dressed as soon as possible and walked to the Lone Oak, a sergeant escorting. There, as I expected, the big soldier known as D'ri was waiting, his canoe in a wagon that stood near. We all mounted the seat, driving pell-mell on a rough road to Tibbals Point, on the southwest corner of Wolf Island. A hard journey it was, and near two o'clock, I should say, before we put our canoe in the water. Then the man D'ri helped me to an easy seat in the bow and shoved off. A full moon, yellow as gold, hung low in the northwest. The water was calm, and we cut across "the moon way," that funnelled off to the shores of Canada.

"It is one ver' gran' night," I said in my dialect of the rude Canuck; for I did not wish him, or any one, to know me. War is war, but, surely, such adventures are not the thing for a woman.

"Yis, mahm," he answered, pushing hard with the paddle. "Yer a friend o' the cap'n, ain't ye — Ray Bell?"

"Ze captain? Ah, oui, m'sieu'," I said. "One ver' brave man, ain't it?"

"Yis, mahm," said he, soberly and with em-

phasis. "He's more 'n a dozen brave men,
thet's whut he is. He's a joemightyful cuss.
Ain't nuthin' he can't dew — spryer 'n a painter,
stouter 'n a moose, an' treemenjous with a
sword."

The moon sank low, peering through distant
tree-columns, and went out of sight. Long
stubs of dead pine loomed in the dim, golden
afterglow, their stark limbs arching high in the
heavens — like mullions in a great Gothic
window.

"When we git nigh shore over yender," said
my companion, "don't believe we better hev a
grea' deal t' say. I ain't a-goin' t' be tuk — by
a jugful — not ef I can help it. Got me 'n a
tight place one night here 'n Canady."

"Ah, m'sieu', in Canada! How did you get
out of it?" I queried.

"Slipped out," said he, shaking the canoe
with suppressed laughter. "Jes' luk a streak
o' greased lightnin'," he added presently.

"The captain he seems ver' anxious for me
to mak' great hurry," I remarked.

"No wonder; it's his lady-love he's efter —
faster 'n a weasel t' see 'er," said he, snickering.

"Good-looking?" I queried.

"Han'some es a pictur'," said he, soberly.

In a moment he dragged his paddle, listening.

"Thet air's th' shore over yender," he whispered. "Don't say a word now. I'll put ye right on the p'int o' rocks. Creep 'long careful till ye git t' th' road, then turn t' th' left, the cap'n tol' me."

When I stepped ashore my dress caught the gunwale and upset our canoe. The good man rolled noisily into the water, and rose dripping. I tried to help him.

"Don't bother me — *none*," he whispered testily, as if out of patience, while he righted the canoe.

When at last he was seated again, as I leaned to shove him off, he whispered in a compensating, kindly manner : "When ye're goin' ashore, an' they's somebody 'n the canoe, don't never try t' tek it with ye 'less ye tell 'im yer goin' tew."

There was a deep silence over wood and water, but he went away so stealthily I could not hear the stir of his paddle. I stood watching as he dimmed off in the darkness, going

quickly out of sight. Then I crept over the
rocks and through a thicket, shivering, for the
night had grown chilly. I snagged my dress
on a brier every step, and had to move by
inches. After mincing along half an hour or
so, I came where I could feel a bit of clear
earth, and stood there, dancing on my tiptoes,
in the dark, to quicken my blood a little. Presently the damp light of dawn came leaking
through the tree-tops. I heard a rattling stir in
the bare limbs above me. Was it some monster
of the woods? Although I have more courage
than most women, it startled me, and I stood
still. The light came clearer; there was a rush
toward me that shook the boughs. I peered
upward. It was only a squirrel, now scratching
his ear, as he looked down at me. He braced
himself, and seemed to curse me loudly for a
spy, trembling with rage and rushing up and
down the branch above me. Then all the
curious, inhospitable folk of the timber-land
came out upon their towers to denounce.

I made my way over the rustling, brittle leaves,
and soon found a trail that led up over high
land. I followed it for a matter of some min-

utes, and came to the road, taking my left-hand way, as they told me. There was no traveller in sight. I walked as fast as I could, passing a village at sunrise, where I asked my way in French at a smithy. Beyond there was a narrow clearing, stumpy and rank with briers, on the up-side of the way. Presently, looking over a level stretch, I could see trees arching the road again, from under which, as I was looking, a squad of cavalry came out in the open. It startled me. I began to think I was trapped. I thought of dodging into the brush. But, no; they had seen me, and I would be a fool now to turn fugitive. I looked about me. Cows were feeding near. I picked up a stick and went deliberately into the bushes, driving one of them to the pike and heading her toward them. They went by at a gallop, never pulling up while in sight of me. Then I passed the cow and went on, stopping an hour later at a lonely log house, where I found French people, and a welcome that included moose meat, a cup of coffee, and fried potatoes. Leaving, I rode some miles with a travelling tinker, a voluble, well-meaning youth who took a liking for me, and went far out of his way to help me on. He blushed proudly when, stopping to mend a pot for the cook at a camp of militia, they inquired if I was his wife.

"No; but she may be yet," said he; "who knows?"

I knew it was no good place for me, and felt some relief when the young man did me this honor. From that moment they set me down for a sweetheart.

"She's too big for you, my boy," said the general, laughing.

"The more the better," said he; "can't have too much of a good wife."

I said little to him as we rode along. He asked for my address, when I left him, and gave me the comforting assurance that he would see me again. I made no answer, leaving him at a turn where, north of us, I could see the white houses of Wrentham. Kingston was hard by, its fort crowning a hill-top by the river.

It was past three by a tower clock at the gate of the Weirs when I got there. A driveway through tall oaks led to the mansion of dark

stone. Many acres of park and field and garden were shut in with high walls. I rang a
bell at the small gate, and some fellow in livery
took my message.

"Wait 'ere, my lass," said he, with an English accent. "I 'll go at once to the secretary."

I sat in a rustic chair by the gate-side, waiting
for that functionary.

"Ah, come in, come in," said he, coolly, as
he opened the gate a little.

He said nothing more, and I followed him —
an oldish man with gray eyes and hair and side-
whiskers, and neatly dressed, his head covered
to the ears with a high hat, tilted backward.
We took a stone path, and soon entered a rear
door.

"She may sit in the servants' hall," said he
to one of the maids.

They took my shawl, as he went away, and
showed me to a room where, evidently, the servants did their eating. They were inquisitive,
those kitchen maids, and now and then I was
rather put to it for a wise reply. I said as
little as might be, using the dialect, long familiar
to me, of the French Canadian. My bonnet

amused them. It was none too new or fashion-
able, and I did not remove it.

"Afraid we 'll steal it," I heard one of them
whisper in the next room. Then there was
a loud laugh.

They gave me a French paper. I read
every line of it, and sat looking out of a
window at the tall trees, at servants who passed
to and fro, at his Lordship's horses, led up and
down for exercise in the stable-yard, at the twi-
light glooming the last pictures of a long day
until they were all smudged with darkness.
Then candle-light, a trying supper hour with
maids and cooks and grooms and footmen
at the big table, English, every one of them,
and set up with haughty curiosity. I would
not go to the table, and had a cup of tea and
a biscuit there in my corner. A big butler
walked in hurriedly awhile after seven. He
looked down at me as if I were the dirt of the
gutter.

"They 're waitin'," said he, curtly. "An'
Sir Chawles would like to know if ye would
care for a humberreller?"

"Ah, m'sieu'! he rains?" I inquired.

"No, mum."

"Ah! he is going to rain, maybe?"

He made no answer, but turned quickly and went to a near closet, from which he brought a faded umbrella.

"There," said he, as he led me to the front door, "see that you send it back."

On the porch were the secretary and the ladies — three of them.

"Ciel! what is it?" one of them whispered as I came out.

The post-lights were shining in their faces, and lovelier I never saw than those of the demoiselles. They stepped lightly to the coach, and the secretary asked if I would go in with them.

"No, m'sieu'," was my answer; "I sit by ze drivaire."

"Come in here, you silly goose," said one of the ladies in French, recognizing my nationality.

"Grand merci!" I said, taking my seat by the driver; and then we were off, with as lively a team as ever carried me, our lights flashing on the tree trunks. We had been riding more than two hours when we stopped for water at a spring-tub under a hill. They gave me a cup, and, for the ladies, I brought each a bumper of the cool, trickling flood.

"Ici, my tall woman," said one of them, presently, "my boot is untied."

Her dainty foot came out of the coach door under ruffles of silk. I hesitated, for I was not accustomed to that sort of service.

"Lambine!" she exclaimed. "Make haste, will you?" her foot moving impatiently.

My fingers had got numb in the cold air, and I must have been very awkward, for presently she boxed my ears and drew her foot away.

"Dieu!" said she. "Tell him to drive on."

I got to my seat quickly, confident that nature had not intended me for a lady's-maid. Awhile later we heard the call of a picket far afield, but saw no camp. A horseman — I thought him a cavalry officer — passed us, flashing in our faces the light of a dark lantern, but said nothing. It must have been near midnight when, as we were going slowly through deep sand, I heard the clang of a cow-bell in the near darkness. Another sounded quickly a bit farther on. The driver gave no heed to it, although I recognized the signal, and knew something would happen shortly. We had come into the double dark of the timber when, suddenly, our horses reared, snorting, and stopped. The driver felt for his big pistol, but not in the right place: for two hours or more it had been stowed away in the deep pocket of my gown. Not a word was spoken. By the dim light of the lanterns we could see men all about us with pikes looming in the dark. For a breath or two there was perfect silence; then the driver rose quickly and shouted: "Who are you?"

"Frien's o' these 'ere women," said one I recognized as the Corporal D'ri.

He spoke in a low tone as he opened the door.

"Grâce au ciel!" I heard one of the young ladies saying. "It is D'ri — dear old fellow!"

Then they all hurried out of the coach and kissed him.

"The captain — is he not here?" said one

of them in French. But D'ri did not understand them, and made no answer.

"Out wi' the lights, an' be still," said D'ri,
quickly, and the lights were out as soon as the
words. "Jones, you tie up a front leg o' one
o' them hosses. Git back in the brush, ladies.
Five on 'em, boys. Now up with the pike
wall!"

From far back in the road had come again
the clang of the cow-bell. I remember hearing
five strokes and then a loud rattle. In a twinkling I was off the seat and beside the ladies.

"Take hold of my dress," I whispered
quickly, "and follow me."

I led them off in the brush, and stopped.
We could hear the move and rattle of cavalry in the near road. Then presently the
swish of steel, the leap and tumble of horses,
the shouting of men. My companions were
of the right stuff; they stood shivering, but
held their peace. Out by the road lights
were flashing, and now we heard pistols and
the sound of a mighty scuffle. I could stay
there in the dark no longer.

"Wait here, and be silent," I said, and ran

"like a madwoman," as they told me long
after, for the flickering lights.

There a squad of cavalry was shut in by
the pikes. Two troopers had broken through
the near line. One had fallen, badly hurt; the
other was sabre to sabre with the man D'ri.
They were close up and striving fiercely, as
if with broadswords. I caught up the weapon
of the injured man, for I saw the Yankee
would get the worst of it. The Britisher
had great power and a sabre quick as a cat's
paw. I could see the corporal was stronger,
but not so quick and skilful. As I stood by,
quivering with excitement, I saw him get a
slash in the shoulder. He stumbled, falling
heavily. Then quickly, forgetting my sex,
but not wholly, I hope, the conduct that becomes a woman, I caught the point of the
sabre, now poised to run him through, with
the one I carried. He backed away, hesi-
tating, for he had seen my hat and gown.
But I made after him with all the fury I
felt, and soon had him in action. He was
tired, I have no doubt; anyway, I whirled his
sabre and broke his hold, whipping it to the

ground. That was the last we saw of him, for he made off in the dark faster than I could follow. The trouble was all over, save the wound of the corporal, which was not as bad as I thought. He was up, and one of them, a surgeon, was putting stitches in his upper arm. Others were tying four men together with rope. Their weapons were lying in a little heap near by. One of the British was saying that Sir Charles Gravleigh had sent for them to ride after the coach.

"Jerushy Jane Pepper!" said the man D'ri. "Never see no sech wil'cat uv a woman es thet air."

I looked down at my gown; I felt of my hat, now hanging over one ear. Sure enough, I was a woman.

"Who be ye, I'd like t' know?" said the man D'ri.

"Ramon Bell — a Yankee soldier of the rank of captain," I said, stripping off my gown. "But, I beg of you, don't tell the ladies I was ever a woman."

"Judas Priest!" said D'ri, as he flung his well arm around me.

FELT foolish for a moment. I had careful plans for Mme. St. Jovite. She would have vanished utterly on our return; so, I fancy, none would have been the wiser. But in that brief sally I had killed the madame; she could serve me no more. I have been careful in my account of this matter to tell all just as it happened, to put upon it neither more nor less of romantic color than we saw. Had I the skill and license of a novelist, I could have made much of my little mystery; but there are many now living who remember all these things, and then, I am a soldier, and too old for a new business. So I make as much of them as there was and no more.

In private theatricals, an evening at the Harbor, I had won applause with the rig, wig, and dialect of my trip to Wrentham Square. So, when I proposed a plan to my friend the general, urging the peril of a raw hand with a trust of so much importance, he had no doubt of my ability.

I borrowed a long coat, having put off my dress, and, when all was ready, went with a lantern to get the ladies. Louise recognized me first.

"Grâce au ciel! le capitaine!" said she, running to meet me.

I dropped my lantern as we came face to face, and have ever been glad of that little accident, for there in the dark my arms went around her, and our lips met for a silent kiss full of history and of holy confidence. Then she put her hand upon my face with a gentle caressing touch, and turned her own away.

"I am very, very glad to see you," I said.

"Dieu!" said her sister, coming near, "we should be glad to see you, if it were possible."

I lighted the lantern hurriedly.

"Ciel! the light becomes him," said Louison, her grand eyes aglow.

But before there was time to answer I had kissed her also.

"He is a bold thing," she added, turning soberly to the baroness.

"Both a bold and happy thing," I answered. "Forgive me. I should not be so bold if I were not — well — insanely happy."

"He is only a boy," said the baroness, laughing as she kissed me.

"Poor little ingénu!" said Louison, patting my arm.

Louise, tall and lovely and sedate as ever, stood near me, primping her bonnet.

"Little ingénu!" she repeated, with a faint laugh of irony as she placed the dainty thing on her head.

"Well, what do *you* think of him?" said Louison, turning to help her.

"Dieu! that he is very big and dreadful," said the other, soberly. "I should think we had better be going."

These things move slowly on paper, but the greeting was to me painfully short, there being of it not more than a minuteful, I should say. On our way to the lights they plied me with whispered queries, and were in fear of more fighting. The prisoners were now in the coach, and our men — there were twelve — stood on every side of it, their pikes in hand. The boats were near, and we hurried to the river by a tote-way. Our schooner lay some twenty rods off a point. A bateau and six canoes were waiting on the beach, and when we had come to the schooner I unbound the prisoners.

"You can get ashore with this bateau," I said. "You will find the horses tied to a tree."

"Wha' does thet mean?" said D'ri.

"That we have no right to hold them," was my answer. "Ronley was in no way respon-sible for their coming."

Leaning over the side with a lantern, while one of our men held the bateau, I motioned to the coachman.

"Give that 'humberreller' to the butler, with my compliments," I whispered.

Our anchors up, our sails took the wind in a jiffy.

"'Member how we used ye," D'ri called to the receding Britishers, "an' ef ye ever meet a Yankee try t' be p'lite tew 'im."

Dawn had come before we got off at the Harbor dock. I took the ladies to an inn for breakfast, wrote a report, and went for my horse and uniform. General Brown was buttoning his suspenders when they admitted me to his room.

"What luck, my boy?" said he.

"All have returned safely, including the ladies," I replied quickly, "and I have the honor to submit a report."

He took a chair, and read the report carefully, and looked up at me, laughing.

"What a lucky and remarkable young man!" said he. "I declare, you should have lived in the Middle Ages"

"Ah, then I should not have enjoyed your compliments or your friendship," was my answer.

He laughed again heartily.

"Nor the demoiselles'," said he. "I congratulate you. They are the loveliest of their sex; but I'm sorry they're not Americans."

"Time enough. I have decided that one of them shall become an American," said I, with all the confidence of youth.

"It is quite an undertaking," said he. "You may find new difficulties. Their father is at the château."

" M'sieur de Lambert ? " I exclaimed.

" M'sieur de Lambert. Came yesterday, via Montreal, with a fine young nobleman — the Count Esmon de Brovel," said he. " You must look out for him; he has the beauty of Apollo and the sword of a cavalier."

" And I no fear of him," I answered soberly, with a quick sense of alarm.

" They rode over in the afternoon with Chaumont," he went on. " It seems the young ladies' father, getting no news of them, had become worried. Well, you may go and have three days for your fun; I shall need you presently."

Breakfast over, I got a team for the ladies, and, mounting my own horse, rode before them. I began to consider a very odd thing in this love experience. While they were in captivity I had begun to think less of Louison and more of Louise. In truth, one face had faded a little in my memory; the other, somehow, had grown clearer and sweeter, as if by a light borrowed from the soul behind it. Now that I saw Louison, her splendid face and figure appealed to me with all the power of old. She was quick,

vivacious, subtle, aggressive, cunning, aware and
proud of her charms, and ever making the most
of them. She, ah, yes, she could play with a
man for the mere pleasure of victory, and be
very heartless if — if she were not in love with
him. This type of woman had no need of argu-
ment to make me feel her charms. With her
the old doubt had returned to me; for how
long? I wondered. Her sister was quite her
antithesis — thoughtful, slow, serious, even-tem-
pered, frank, quiet, unconscious of her beauty,
and with that wonderful thing, a voice tender
and low and sympathetic and full of an elo-
quence I could never understand, although I
felt it to my finger-tips. I could not help loving
her, and, indeed, what man with any life in him
feels not the power of such a woman? That
morning, on the woods-pike, I reduced the problem to its simplest terms: the one was a physical
type, the other a spiritual.

"M'sieur le Capitaine," said Louison, as I
rode by the carriage, "what became of the tall
woman last night?"

"Left us there in the woods," I answered.
"She was afraid of you."

" Afraid of me! Why?"

"Well, I understand that you boxed her ears shamefully."

A merry peal of laughter greeted my words.

"It was too bad; you were very harsh," said Louise, soberly.

"I could not help it; she was an ugly, awkward thing," said Louison. "I could have pulled her nose."

"And it seems you called her a géante also," I said. "She was quite offended."

"It was a compliment," said the girl. "She was an Amazon — like the count's statue of Jeanne d'Arc."

"Poor thing! she could not help it," said Louise.

"Well," said Louison, with a sigh of regret, "if I ever see her again I shall give her a five-franc piece."

There was a moment of silence, and she broke it.

"I hope, this afternoon, you will let me ride that horse," said she.

"On one condition," was my reply.

"And it is — ?"

"That you will let me ride yours at the same time."

"Agreed," was her answer. "Shall we go at three?"

"With the consent of the baroness and — and your father," I said.

"Father!" exclaimed the two girls.

"Your father," I repeated. "He is now at the château."

"Heavens!" said Louison.

"What will he say?" said the baroness.

"I am so glad — my dear papa!" said Louise, clapping her hands.

We were out of the woods now, and could see the château in the uplands.

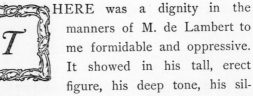HERE was a dignity in the manners of M. de Lambert to me formidable and oppressive. It showed in his tall, erect figure, his deep tone, his silvered hair and mustache. There was a merry word between the kisses of one daughter; between those of the other only tears and a broken murmur.

"Oh, papa," said Louison, as she greeted him, "I do love you — but I dread that — tickly old mustache. Mon Dieu! what a lover — you must have been!"

Then she presented me, and put her hand upon my arm, looking proudly at her father.

"My captain!" said she. "Did you ever see a handsomer Frenchman?"

"There are many, and here is one," said he, turning to the young count, who stood behind him — a fine youth, tall, strong-built, well-spoken, with blond hair and dark, keen eyes. I admit frankly I had not seen a better figure of a man. I assure you, he had the form of Hercules, the eye of Mars. It was an eye to command — women; for I had small reason to admire his courage when I knew him better. He took a hand of each young lady, and kissed it with admirable gallantry.

"Dieu! it is not so easy always to agree with one's father," said Louison.

We went riding that afternoon — Thérèse and her marquis and Louison and I. The first two went on ahead of us; we rode slowly, and for a time no word was spoken. Winds had stripped the timber, and swept its harvest to the walls and hollows, where it lay bleaching in the sun. Birch and oak and maple were holding bared arms to the wind, as if to toughen them for storm and stress. I felt a mighty sadness, wondering if my own arms were quite seasoned for all that was to come. The merry-hearted girl beside me was ever like a day of June — the color of the rose in her cheek, its odor always in her hair and lace. There was never an hour of autumn in her life.

"Alas, you are a very silent man!" said she, presently, with a little sigh.

"Only thinking," I said.

"Of what?"

"Dieu! of the dead summer," I continued.

"Believe me, it does not pay to think," she interrupted. "I tried it once, and made a sad discovery."

"Of what?"

"A fool!" said she, laughing.

"I should think it — it might have been a coquette," said I, lightly.

"Why, upon my word," said she, "I believe you misjudge me. Do you think me heartless?"

For the first time I saw a shadow in her face.

"No; but you are young and — and beautiful, and —"

"What?" she broke in impatiently, as I hesitated. "I long to know."

"Men will love you in spite of all you can do," I added.

"Captain!" said she, turning her face away.

"Many will love you, and — and you can choose only one — a very hard thing to do — possibly."

" Not hard," said she, " if I see the right one
— and — and — he loves me also."

I had kept myself well in hand, for I was full
of doubts that day; but the clever girl came
near taking me, horse, foot, and guns, that
moment. She spoke so charmingly, she looked
so winning, and then, was it not easy to ask if I
were the lucky one ? She knew I loved her, I
knew that she *had* loved me, and I might as well
confess. But no ; I was not ready.

" You must be stern with the others; you
must not let them tell you," I went on.

" Ciel ! " said she, laughing, " one might as
well go to a nunnery. May not a girl enjoy her
beauty ? It is sweet to her."

" But do not make it bitter for the poor men.
Dieu ! I am one of them, and know their
sorrows."

" And you — you have been in love ? "

" Desperately," I answered, clinging by the
finger-tips. Somehow we kept drifting into fate-
ful moments when a word even might have
changed all that has been — our life way, the
skies above us, the friends we have known, our
loves, our very souls.

She turned, smiling, her beauty flashing up at
me with a power quite irresistible. I shut my
eyes a moment, summoning all my forces.
There was only a step between me and — God
knows what!

"Captain, you are a foolish fellow," said she,
with a little shudder. "And I — well, I am
cold. Parbleu! feel my hand."

She had drawn her glove quickly, and held
out her hand, white and beautiful, a dainty
finger in a gorget of gems. That little cold,
trembling hand seemed to lay hold of my heart
and pull me to her. As my lips touched the
palm I felt its mighty magic. Dear girl! I wonder if she planned that trial for me.

"We must — ride — faster. You — you —
are cold," I stammered.

She held her hand so that the sunlight
flashed in the jewels, and looked down upon
it proudly.

"Do you think it beautiful?" she asked.

"Yes, and wonderful," I said. "But, mark
me, it is all a sacred trust — the beauty you
have."

"Sacred?"

"More sacred than the power of kings," I said.

"Preacher!" said she, with a smile. "You should give yourself to the church."

"I can do better with the sword of steel," I said.

"But do not be sad. Cheer up, dear fellow!" she went on, patting my elbow with a pretty mockery. "We women are not — not so bad. When I find the man I love —"

Her voice faltered as she began fussing with her stirrup.

I turned with a look of inquiry, changing quickly to one of admiration.

"I shall make him love *me*, if I can," she went on soberly.

"And if he does?" I queried, my blood quickening as our eyes met.

"Dieu! I would do anything for him," said she.

I turned away, looking off at the brown fields. Ah, then, for a breath, my heart begged my will for utterance. The first word passed my lips when there came a sound of galloping hoofs and Thérèse and the marquis.

"Come, dreamers," said the former, as they pulled up beside us. "A cold dinner is the worst enemy of happiness."

"And he is the worst robber that shortens the hour of love," said the marquis, smiling.

We turned, following them at a swift gallop. They had helped me out of that mire of ecstasy, and now I was glad, for, on my soul, I believed the fair girl had found one more to her liking, and was only playing for my scalp. And at last I had begun to know my own heart, or thought I had.

D'ri came over that evening with a letter from General Brown. He desired me to report for duty next day at two.

"War — it is forever war," said Thérèse, when I told her at dinner. "There is to be a coaching-party to-morrow, and we shall miss you, captain."

"Can you not soon return?" said the baroness.

"I fear not," was my answer. "It is to be a long campaign."

"Oh, the war! When will it ever end?" said Louise, sighing.

"When we are all dead," said Louison.

"Of loneliness?" said the old count, with a smile.

"No; of old age," said Louison, quickly.

"When the army goes into Canada it will go into trouble," said the Comte de Chaumont, speaking in French. "We shall have to get you out of captivity, captain."

"Louise would rescue him," said her sister. "She has influence there."

"Would you pay my ransom?" I inquired, turning to her.

"With my life," said she, solemnly.

"Greater love hath no man than this," said the good Père Joulin, smiling as the others laughed.

"And none has greater obligation," said Louise, blushing with embarrassment. "Has he not brought us three out of captivity?"

"Well, if I am taken," I said, "nothing can bring me back unless it be — "

"A miracle?" the baroness prompted as I paused.

"Yes; even a resurrection," was my answer. "I know what it means for a man to be captured there these days."

Louise sat beside me, and I saw what others failed to notice — her napkin stop quickly on its way to her lips, her hand tighten as it held the white linen. It made me regretful of my thoughtless answer, but oddly happy for a moment. Then they all besought me for some adventure of those old days in the army. I told them the story of the wasps, and, when I had finished, our baroness told of the trouble it led to — their capture and imprisonment.

"It was very strange," said she, in conclusion. "That Englishman grew kinder every day we were there, until we began to feel at home."

They were all mystified, but I thought I could understand it. We had a long evening of music, and I bade them all good-by before going to bed, for they were to be off early.

Well, the morning came clear, and before I was out of bed I heard the coach-horn, the merry laughter of ladies under my window, the prancing hoofs, and the crack of the whip as they all went away. It surprised me greatly to find Louise at the breakfast table when I came below-stairs; I shall not try to say how much it pleased me. She was gowned in pink, a red rose at her bosom. I remember, as if it were yesterday, the brightness of her big eyes, the glow in her cheeks, the sweet dignity of her tall, fine figure when she rose and gave me her hand.

"I did feel sorry, ma'm'selle, that I could not go; but now — now I am happy," was my remark.

"Oh, captain, you are very gallant," said she, as we took seats. "I was not in the mood for merrymaking, and then, I am reading a book."

"A book! May its covers be the gates of happiness," I answered.

"Eh bien! it is a tale of love," said she.

"Of a man for a woman?" I inquired.

"Of a lady that loved two knights, and knew not which the better."

"Is it possible and — and reasonable?" I inquired. "In a tale things should go as — well, as God plans them."

"Quite possible," said she, "for in such a thing as love who knows what — what may happen?"

"Except he have a wide experience," I answered.

"And have God's eyes," said she. "Let me tell you. They were both handsome, brave, splendid, of course, but there was a difference: the one had a more perfect beauty of form and face, the other a nobler soul."

"And which will she favor?"

"Alas! I have not read, and do not know her enough to judge," was her answer; "but I shall hate her if she does not take him with the better soul."

"And why?" I could hear my heart beating.

"Love is not love unless it be—" She paused, thinking. "Dieu! from soul to soul," she added feelingly.

She was looking down, a white, tapered finger stirring the red petals of the rose. Then she spoke in a low, sweet tone that trembled with holy feeling and cut me like a sword of the spirit going to its very hilt in my soul.

"Love looks to what is noble," said she, "or it is vain—it is wicked; it fails; it dies in a day, like the rose. True love, that is forever."

"What if it be hopeless?" I whispered.

"Ah! then it is very bitter," said she, her

voice diminishing. "It may kill the body, but
—but love does not die. When it comes—"

There was a breath of silence that had in it
a strange harmony not of this world.

"'When it comes'?" I whispered.

"You see the coming of a great king," said
she, looking down thoughtfully, her chin upon
her hand.

"And all people bow their heads," I said.

"Yes," she added, with a sigh, "and give
their bodies to be burned, if he ask it. The
king is cruel—sometimes."

"Dieu!" said I. "He has many captives."

She broke a sprig of fern, twirling it in her
fingers; her big eyes looked up at me, and saw,
I know, to the bottom of my soul.

"But long live the king!" said she, her lips
trembling, her cheeks as red as the rose upon
her bosom.

"Long live the king!" I murmured.

We dared go no farther. Sweet philosopher,
inspired of Heaven, I could not bear the look
of her, and rose quickly with dim eyes and went
out of the open door. A revelation had come
to me. Mère de Dieu! how I loved that

woman so fashioned in thy image! She followed me, and laid her hand upon my arm tenderly, while I shook with emotion.

"Captain," said she, in that sweet voice,
"captain, what have I done?"

It was the first day of the Indian summer,
a memorable season that year, when, according
to an old legend, the Great Father sits idly on
the mountain-tops and blows the smoke of his
long pipe into the valleys. In a moment I was
quite calm, and stood looking off to the hazy
hollows of the far field. I gave her my arm
without speaking, and we walked slowly down
a garden path. For a time neither broke the
silence.

"I did not know — I did not know," she
whispered presently.

"And I — must — tell you," I said brokenly,
"that I — that I — "

"Hush-sh-sh!" she whispered, her hand
over my lips. "Say no more! say no more!
If it is true, go — go quickly, I beg of
you!"

There was such a note of pleading in her
voice, I hear it, after all this long time, in the

hushed moments of my life, night or day. " Go
— go quickly, I beg of you!" We were both
near breaking down.

" Vive le roi!" I whispered, taking her hand.

" Vive le roi!" she whispered, turning away.

OW empty and weak are my words that try to tell of that day! I doubt if there is in them anywhere what may suggest, even feebly, the height and depth of that experience or one ray of the light in her face. There are the words nearly as we said them; there are the sighs, the glances, the tears: but everywhere there is much missing — that fair young face and a thousand things irresistible that drift in with every tide of high feeling. Of my history there is not much more to write, albeit some say the best is untold.

I had never such a heart of lead as went with me to my work that afternoon. What became of me I cared not a straw then, for I knew my love was hopeless. D'ri met me as I got off my horse at the Harbor. His keen eye saw my trouble quickly — saw near to the bottom of it.

"Be'n hit?" said he, his great hand on my shoulder.

"With trouble," I answered. "Torn me up a little inside."

"Thought so," he remarked soberly. "Judas Priest! ye luk es ef a shell 'ad bu'st 'n yer cockpit. Ain' nuthin' 'll spile a man quicker. Sheer off a leetle an' git out o' range. An' 'member, Ray, don't never give up the ship. Thet air 's whut Perry tol' us."

I said nothing and walked away, but have always remembered his counsel, there was so much of his big heart in it. The army was to move immediately, in that foolish campaign of Wilkinson that ended with disaster at Chrysler's Farm. They were making the boats, small craft with oars, of which three hundred or more would be needed to carry us. We were to go eastward on the river and join Hampden, whose corps was to march overland to Plattsburg, at some point on the north shore. Word came, while I was away, that down among the islands our enemy had been mounting cannon. It looked as if our plan had leaked, as if, indeed, there were good chance of our being blown out of water the first day of our journey. So, before the army started, I was to take D'ri and eleven others, with four boats, and go down to reconnoitre.

We got away before sundown that day, and, as dark came, were passing the southwest corner of Wolf Island. I was leading the little fleet, and got ashore, intending to creep along the edge and rejoin them at the foot of the island. I had a cow-bell, muted with cork, and was to clang it for a signal in case of need. Well, I was a bit more reckless that night than ever I had been. Before I had gone twenty rods I warned them to flee and leave me. I heard a move in the brush, and was backing off, when a light flashed on me, and I felt the touch of a bayonet. Then quickly I saw there was no help for me, and gave the signal, for I was walled in. Well, I am not going to tell the story of my capture. My sabre could serve me well, but, heavens! it was no magic wand such as one may read of in the story-books. I knew then it would serve me best in the scabbard.

There were few words and no fighting in the ceremony. I gave up, and let them bind my arms. In two hours they had me in jail, I knew not where. In the morning they let me send a note to Lord Ronley, who was now barely two days out of his own trouble. A week passed; I was to be tried for a spy, and saw clearly the end of it all. Suddenly, a morning when my hopes were gone, I heard the voice of his Lordship in the little corridor. A keeper came with him to the door of my cell, and opened it.

"The doctor," said he.

"Well, well, old fellow," said Ronley, clapping me on the shoulder, "you are ill, I hear."

"Really, I do not wish to alarm you," I said, smiling, "but — but it does look serious."

He asked me to show my tongue, and I did so.

"Cheer up," said he, presently; "I have brought you this pill. It is an excellent remedy."

He had taken from his pocket a brown pill of the size of a large pea, and sat rolling it in his palm. Had he brought me poison?

"I suppose it is better than —"

He shot a glance at me as if to command silence, then he put the pill in my palm. I saw it was of brown tissue rolled tightly.

"Don't take it now," said he; "too soon after breakfast. Wait half an hour. A cup of water," he added, turning to the guard, who left us for a moment.

He leaned to my ear and whispered: —

"Remember," said he, "2 is *a*, and 3 is *b*, and so on. Be careful until the guard changes."

He handed me a small watch as he was leaving.

"It may be good company," he remarked.

I unrolled the tissue as soon as I was alone. It was covered with these figures: —

21-24-6-13-23-6

21-16-15-10-8-9-21 4-6-13-13 5-16-16-19 22-15-13-16-4-12-6-5 13-10-7-21 20-14-2-13-13 24-10-15-5-16-24 10-15 4-16-19-19-10-5-16-19 3-2-4-12 21-16 24-2-13-13 8-16 19-10-8-9-21 21-16 19-16-2-5 13-6-7-21 200 17-2-4-6-20 21-16 17-2-21-9 13-6-7-21 21-16 19-10-23-6-19 19-10-8-9-21 21-24-6-15-21-26 21-16 21-9-10-4-12-6-21.

I made out the reading, shortly, as follows : —

"Twelve to-night cell door unlocked. Lift small window in corridor. Back to wall go right to road. Left two hundred paces to path. Left to river. Right twenty to thicket."

Having read the figures, I rolled the tissue firmly, and hid it in my ear. It was a day of some excitement, I remember, for that very afternoon I was condemned to death. A priest, having heard of my plight, came in that evening, and offered me the good ministry of the church. The words, the face, of that simple man, filled me with a deep tenderness for all who seek in the shadows of this world with the lantern of God's mercy. Never, so long as I live, shall an ill word of them go unrebuked in my hearing. He left me at 10.30, and as he went away, my jailer banged the iron door without locking it. Then I lay down there in the dark, and began to tell off the time by my heart-beats, allowing forty-five hundred to the hour, and was not far wrong. I thought much of his Lordship as I waited. To him I had been of some service, but, surely, not enough to explain this tender regard, involving, as it must have done, bribery and no small degree of peril to himself. My counting over, I tried the door, which swung easily as I put my hand upon it. The little corridor was dark and I could hear no sound save the snoring of a drunken soldier, committed that day for fighting, as the turnkey had told me. I found the small window, and slid the sash, and let my boots fall to the ground, then climbing through and dropping on them. It was a dark night, but I was not long in reaching the road and pacing my way to the path and river. His Lordship and a boatman lay in the thicket waiting for me.

"This way," the former whispered, taking my arm and leading me to the mouth of a little brook, where a boat was tied, the bottom muffled with blankets. I took the stern seat, his Lordship the bow, and we pushed off. The boatman, a big, husky fellow, had been rowing a long hour when we put into a cove under the high shore of an island. I could see a moving glow back in the bushes. It swung slowly, like a pendulum of light, with a mighty flit and tumble of shadows. We tied our boat, climbed the shore, and made slowly for the light. Nearing it, his Lordship whistled twice, and got answer. The lantern was now still; it lighted the side of a soldier in high boots; and suddenly I saw it was D'ri. I caught his hand, raising it to my lips. We could not speak, either of us. He stepped aside, lifting the lantern. God! there stood Louise. She was all in black, her head bent forward.

"Dear love!" I cried, grasping her hands, "why — why have you come here?"

She turned her face away, and spoke slowly, her voice trembling with emotion.

"To give my body to be burned," said she.

I turned, lifting my arm to smite the man who had brought me there; but lo! some stronger hand had struck him, some wonder-working power of a kind that removes mountains. Lord Ronley was wiping his eyes.

"I cannot do this thing," said he, in a broken voice. "I cannot do this thing. Take her and go."

D'ri had turned away to hide his feelings.

"Take them to your boat," said his Lordship.

"Wait a minute," said D'ri, fixing his lantern.

"Judas Priest! I ain't got no stren'th. I 'm all tore t' shoe-strings."

I took her arm, and we followed D'ri to the landing, Lord Ronley coming with us.

"Good-by," said he, leaning to push us off. "I am a better man for knowing you. Dear girl, you have put all the evil out of me."

He held a moment to the boat, taking my hand as I came by him.

"Bell," said he, "henceforward may there be peace between you and me."

"And between your country and mine," I answered.

And, thank God! the war was soon over, and ever since there has been peace between the two great peoples. I rejoice that even we old men have washed our hearts of bitterness, and that the young have now more sense of brotherhood.

Above all price are the words of a wise man, but silence, that is the great counsellor. In silence wisdom enters the heart and understanding puts forth her voice. In the hush of that night ride I grew to manhood; I put away childish things. I saw, or thought I saw, the two great powers of good and evil. One was love, with the power of God in it to lift up, to ennoble; the other, love's counterfeit, a cunning device of the devil, with all his power to wreck and destroy, deceiving him that has taken it until he finds at last he has neither gold nor silver, but only base metal hanging as a millstone to his neck.

At dawn we got ashore on Battle Point. We waited there, Louise and I, while D'ri went away to bring horses. The sun rose clear and warm; it was like a summer morning, but stiller, for the woods had lost their songful tenantry. We took the forest road, walking slowly. Some bugler near us had begun to play the song of Yankee-land. Its phrases travelled like waves in the sea, some high-crested, moving with a mighty rush, filling the valleys, mounting the hills, tossing their spray aloft, flooding all the shores of silence. Far and near, the trees were singing in praise of my native land.

"Ramon," said Louise, looking up at me, a sweet and queenly dignity in her face, "I have come to love this country."

"And you could not have done so much for me unless you had loved — "

She looked up at me quickly, and put her finger to her lips. My tongue faltered, obeying the command. How sweet and beautiful she was then, her splendid form erect, the light of her eyes softened by long lashes! She looked down thoughtfully as she gave the bottom of her gown a shake.

"Once upon a time," said she, slowly, as our eyes met again, "there was a little country that had a cruel king. And he commanded that none of all his people should speak until — until —"

She hesitated, stirring the dead leaves with her dainty foot.

"Until a great mountain had been removed and buried in the sea," she added in a low tone.

"Ah, that was hard."

"Especially for the ladies," she went on, sighing. "Dieu! they could only sit and hold their tongues and weep and feel very foolish. And the longer they were silent the more they had to say."

"And those who broke the law?" I inquired.

"Were condemned to silence for their lives,"

she answered. " Come, we are both in danger;
let us go."

A bit farther on we came to a log house
where a veteran of the old war sat playing his
bugle, and a motherly woman bade us sit awhile
at the door-step.

'RI came soon with horses, one the black thoroughbred of Louise which had brought her on this errand. We gave them free rein, heading for the château. Not far up the woods-pike we met M. de Lambert and the old count. The former was angry, albeit he held himself in hand as became a gentleman, save that he was a bit too cool with me.

"My girl, you have upset us terribly," said the learned doctor. "I should like to be honored with your confidence."

"And I with your kindness, dear father," said she, as her tears began falling. "I am much in need of it."

"She has saved my life, m'sieur," I said.

"Then go to your work," said he, coolly, "and make the most of it."

"Ah, sir, I had rather —"

"Good-by," said Louise, giving me her hand.

"Au revoir," I said quickly, and wheeled my horse and rode away.

The boats were ready. The army was waiting for the order, now expected any moment, to move. General Brown had not been at his quarters for a day.

"Judas Priest!" said D'ri, when we were alone together, "thet air gal 'd go through fire an' water fer you."

"You 're mistaken," I said.

"No, I hain't nuther," said he. "Ef I be, I 'm a reg'lar out-an'-out fool, hand over fist."

He whittled a moment thoughtfully.

"Ain' no use talkin'," he added, "I can tell a hoss from a jack-rabbit any day."

"Her father does not like me," I suggested.

"Don't hev to," said D'ri, calmly.

He cut a deep slash in the stick he held, then added: "Don't make no odds ner no dif-f'rence one way er t' other. I did n't like th' measles, but I hed t' hev 'em."

"He 'll never permit a marriage with me," I said.

"'T ain't nec'sary," he declared soberly. "In this 'ere country don' tek only tew t' mek a bargain. One o' the blessin's o' liberty."

He squinted up at the sky, delivering his confidence in slowly measured phrases, to wit:

"Wouldn't give ten cents fer no man 'at 'll give up a gal 'less he 'd orter — not fer nuthin' ner nobody."

I was called out of bed at cockcrow in the morning. The baroness and a footman were at the door.

"Ah, my captain, there is trouble," she whispered. "M. de Lambert has taken his daughters. They are going back to Paris, bag and baggage. Left in the evening."

"By what road?"

"The turnpike militaire."

"Thanks, and good morning," I said. "I shall overhaul them."

I called D'ri, and bade him feed the horses quickly. I went to see General Brown, but he and Wilkinson were on the latter's gig, half a mile out in the harbor. I scribbled a note to the farmer-general, and, leaving it, ran to the stables. Our horses were soon ready, and D'ri and I were off a bit after daylight, urging up hill and down at a swift gallop, and making the forest ring with hoof-beats. Far beyond the château we slackened pace and went along leisurely. Soon we passed the town where they had put up overnight, and could see the tracks of horse and coach-wheel. D'ri got off and examined them presently.

" Purty fresh," he remarked. " Can't be more 'n five mild er so further on."

We rode awhile in silence.

" How ye goin' t' tackle 'em?" he inquired presently.

" Going to stop them somehow," said I, "and get a little information."

" An' mebbe a gal?" he suggested.

" Maybe a gal."

" Don' care s' long as ye dew th' talkin'. I can rassle er fight, but my talk in a rumpus ain' fit fer no woman t' hear, thet 's sart'in."

We overtook the coach at a village, near ten o'clock.

D'ri rushed on ahead of them, wheeling with drawn sabre. The driver pulled rein, stopping quickly. M. de Lambert was on the seat beside him. I came alongside.

"Then I leave all for you."

"Robbers!" said M. de Lambert. "What do you mean?"

The young ladies and Brovel were looking out of the door, Louise pale and troubled.

"No harm to any, m'sieur," I answered. "Put up your pistol."

I opened the coach door. M. de Lambert, hissing with anger, leaped to the road. I knew he would shoot me, and was making ready to close with him, when I heard a rustle of silk, and saw Louise between us, her tall form erect, her eyes forceful and commanding. She stepped quickly to her father.

"Let me have it!" said she, taking the pistol from his hand. She flung it above the heads of some village folk who had gathered near us.

"Why do you stop us?" she whispered, turning to me.

"So you may choose between him and me," I answered.

"Then I leave all for you," said she, coming quickly to my side.

The villagers began to cheer, and old D'ri flung his hat in the air, shouting, "Hurrah fer love an' freedom!"

"An' the United States of Ameriky," some one added.

"She is my daughter," said M. de Lambert, with anger, as he came up to me. "I may command her, and I shall seek the aid of the law as soon as I find a magistrate."

"But see that you find him before we find a minister," I said.

"The dominie! Here he is," said some one near us.

"Marry them," said another. "It is Captain Bell of the army, a brave and honorable man."

Does not true love, wherever seen, spread its own quality and prosper by the sympathy it commands? Louise turned to the good man, taking his hand.

"Come," said she, "there is no time to lose."

The minister came to our help. He could not resist her appeal, so sweetly spoken. There, under an elm by the wayside, with some score of witnesses, including Louison and the young Comte de Brovel, who came out of the coach and stood near, he made us man and wife. We were never so happy as when we stood there hand in hand, that sunny morning, and heard the prayer for God's blessing, and felt a mighty uplift in our hearts. As to my sweetheart, there was never such a glow in her cheeks, such a light in her large eyes, such a grace in her figure.

"Dear sister," said Louison, kissing her, "I wish I were as happy."

"And you shall be as soon as you get to Paris," said the young count.

"Oh, dear, I can hardly wait!" said the merry-hearted girl, looking proudly at her new lover.

"I admire your pluck, my young man," said M. de Lambert, as we shook hands. "You Americans are a great people. I surrender; I am not going to be foolish. Turn your horses," said he, motioning to the driver. "We shall go back at once."

I helped Louise into the coach with her sister and the Comte de Brovel. D'ri and I rode on behind them, the village folk cheering and waving their hats.

"Ye done it skilful," said D'ri, smiling. "Whut 'd I tell ye?"

I made no answer, being too full of happiness at the moment.

"Tell ye one thing, Ray," he went on soberly: "ef a boy an' a gal loves one 'nother, an' he has any grit in 'im, can't nuthin' keep 'em apart long."

He straightened the mane of his horse, and then added: —

"Ner they can't nuthin' conquer 'em."

Soon after two o'clock we turned in at the château.

We were a merry company at luncheon, the doctor drinking our health and happiness with sublime resignation. But I had to hurry back — that was the worst of it all. Louise walked with me to the big gate, where were D'ri and the horses. We stopped a moment on the way.

"Again?" she whispered, her sweet face on my shoulder. "Yes, and as often as you like. No more now — there is D'ri. Remember, sweetheart, I shall look and pray for you day and night."

OONER or later all things come
to an end, including wars and
histories, — a God's mercy! —
and even the lives of such lucky
men as I. All things, did I say?
Well, what wonder, for am I not writing of
youth and far delights with a hand trembling
of infirmity? All things save one, I meant
to say, and that is love, the immortal vine,
with its root in the green earth, that weathers
every storm, and "groweth not old," and climbs
to paradise; and who eats of its fruit has in him
ever a thought of heaven — a hope immortal as
itself.

This book of my life ends on a bright morning in the summer of '17, at the new home of
James Donatianus Le Ray, Comte de Chaumont, the château having burned the year
before.

President Monroe is coming on the woods-pike, and veterans are drawn up in line to meet him. Here are men who fought at Chippewa and Lundy's Lane and Lake Erie and Chrysler's Farm, and here are some old chaps who fought long before at Plattsburg and Ticonderoga. Joseph Bonaparte, the ex-king of Spain, so like his mighty brother at St. Helena, is passing the line. He steps proudly, in ruffles and green velvet. Gondolas with liveried gondoliers, and filled with fair women, are floating on the still lake, now rich with shadow-pictures of wood and sky and rocky shore.

A burst of melody rings in the great harp of the woodland. In that trumpet peal, it seems, a million voices sing: —

Hail, Columbia, happy land!

Slowly the line begins to limp along. There are wooden legs and crutches and empty sleeves in that column. D'ri goes limping in front, his right leg gone at the knee since our last charge. Draped around him is that old battle-flag of the *Lawrence*. I march beside him, with only this long seam across my cheek to show that I had been with him that bloody day at Chrysler's. We move slowly over a green field to the edge of the forest. There, in the cool shadow, are ladies in white, and long tables set for a feast. My dear wife, loved of all and more beautiful than ever, comes to meet us.

"Sweetheart," she whispers, "I was never so proud to be your wife."

"And an American," I suggest, kissing her.

"And an American," she answers.

A bugle sounds; the cavalcade is coming.

"The President!" they cry, and we all begin cheering.

He leads the escort on a black horse, a fine figure in military coat and white trousers, his cocked hat in hand, a smile lighting his face. The count receives him and speaks our welcome. President Monroe looks down the war-scarred line a moment. His eyes fill with tears, and then he speaks to us.

"Sons of the woodsmen," says he, concluding his remarks, "you shall live in the history of a greater land than that we now behold or dream of, and in the gratitude of generations yet unborn, long, long after we are turned to dust."

And then we all sing loudly with full hearts:

O land I love ! — thy acres sown
With sweat and blood and shattered bone —
God's grain, that ever doth increase
The goodly harvest of his peace.

D'RI AND I